A KISS IN DARKNESS
Novella

CAROL GOODNIGHT

Copyright © 2017 Carol Goodnight

All rights reserved.

ISBN: 978-0-9971528-

Mike

Resting near the ancient oak
On fresh cut grass he often lay
Spirits of the child halt
To watch a cloud of dragon play

Called to grace another place
When day left all too soon
He stopped to catch a firefly
Then watch the night bewitch the moon

So listen now the rustling breeze
As one by one caress the sky
His fleeting fading shadow gone
To ever soar where eagles fly

Carol Goodnight

ACKNOWLEDGMENTS

Kelly Williamson

Aidan Ruth

Lily Burhenne

Howie Fries (BigH)

Patricia Pahula

James Brindley

This book is a work of fiction. Names, characters, places and incidents either are the product of the author's imagination or are used fictitiously. Any resemblance to actual persons, living or dead, or to actual events or locales is entirely coincidental.

A KISS IN DARKNESS

CAROL GOODNIGHT

CHAPTER 1

Even before she registered what the caller was saying, a loss so great it would haunt her in varied ways for the rest of her life sucker punched her in the gut.

"Your brother is dead," said the trembling voice on the other end of the phone.

Carolyn Wingate floundered for a response.

"Mike's dead," the voice repeated.

***

Northern Virginia

Seven sweat-glistening honor guards took their stance and aimed their M1 rifles into the cloudless sky on that blistering August afternoon. They fired three synchronized rounds, manually cycling the action. As each volley rang out, Carolyn jerked, wounded every bit as much had those blasts pierced her body instead of just her soul. An itchy bead of sweat trickled down her left temple as she watched wispy coils of smoke rise from the rifle tips, linger, and then drift away. Singed gunpowder burned her nose and her throat ached.

Can your palate break from holding back tears, she wondered as her gaze fixed on the dissipating smoke.

She'd never been a crier. But the death of her brother had been the beginning of many changes for Carolyn Wingate.

The sound of Taps moaning from the bugle broke her final grasp on composure. The gleaming brass buttons and medals with the somber lone bugle glinted through her tears as they tumbled over the well-worn path on her cheeks.

"Day is done."

The languid, melancholy notes echoed over the neat, crisp-baked edges of the manicured lawn and into the deep shadow of limp leaves hanging from an old stand of far-off cottonwood trees.

Her brother was gone. The final thread that held her life together had come undone.

Carolyn slunk deeper into the hard wooden chair and tried to focus on the pain in her back—anything other than what was happening.

She'd never been a wisher either. She was a doer. But she was wishing now. She was wishing she didn't exist. That she'd never existed. She didn't want to be here, and she didn't want to do this. At the same time, she wished things were back to normal, that her mother was still alive, or even her real father. But they'd both been gone for years. In every part of the now-empty space in her heart, she knew she'd never know normal again.

He'd been on assignment in Istanbul. They'd told her it was a car accident. A terrible crash on a bridge. Senseless. Tragic. She hadn't asked for details. She couldn't bear to hear them. She already knew the most important thing. He was gone.

A pair of pristine dress-white parade gloves slipped three spent bullet casings into the folded flag before presenting it to her. She was the only immediate family left. She closed her eyes and clutched the flag to her heart as if it contained her brother's spirit. The lightness of the fabric in her arms disturbed her.

Mike's friends and coworkers hovered over her, telling her what a great guy he'd been. She listened as she strained to keep from sobbing. She appreciated that they'd arranged this memorial service even if it had meant a long drive.

Several of them had funny stories about a prank or two they'd pulled on each other in their many lonely off-hours. As the morning wore on, one by one, they bent and shook her hand before leaving.

Mike would've laughed. He would've said she was playing the part of the queen she always fantasized being. All of these subjects, here at his behest, were bowing to her at court. He was always trying to get her to come out of her shell.

One large man stood off to the side pacing around the edge of the building. Although he fit in with the military look, he wore civilian clothes and didn't seem to know the others. She felt his eyes fixed on her through most of the ceremony, but he never approached. She thought he might have been building maintenance.

As the last of the group left, the cloying fragrance and vibrant colors of the many floral arrangements drew Carolyn to the podium. Mesmerized by the buds, young and bursting with life, the knot in her throat tightened again. She reached to touch the silky petals as their stalks, already limp from the summer heat, evoked a reminder that the glory once promised from these tight, swelling blossoms would never unfurl.

Before she left, she plucked a perfect white rose from amongst the wilting bouquets. The lovely fragrance, her lone companion now, trailed behind as she stepped toward her car.

The large man rushed from behind the building. His free arm

gestured in frustration as he held the phone to his ear and headed toward the out-lot parking area. His bulky shoulders leaning forward gave his gait the appearance of a sinister cartoon character.

He must have been waiting for her to leave, and as she watched him plodding toward his car, she felt a little guilty for lingering.

A strange, low-pitched groan reverberated through her chest before escaping her throat in an unrecognizable sound as she drove west on Dolley Madison Blvd. past the CIA headquarters in Langley, Virginia.

Behind the silent gusting leaves, past the young serious faced guards, and beyond the massive circular Central Intelligence insignia set in the floor, the lobby held a stainless steel frame topped by an inch-thick plate of bulletproof glass. In the case lay the Book of Honor. They would add a new star to the book that day. His star.

The bit of colorful cloth she'd received and that star were all that remained of her brother. An empty, dark void crept through her.

A memory of her brother's Cheshire grin flashed in her mind. Even as a child he would enter a room, take in his surroundings before raising his eyebrow a hitch, and give her that knowing grin. The smugness from his inner humor always gave him away. Something was about to happen, either terrible or fantastic, depending on your perspective, that usually left them both doubled over in laughter.

A tear rolled down her cheek as she pulled off the interstate into a leafy suburb where the residents, most likely eating salads or folding laundry, remained unaware that catastrophe could pay them a visit at any moment. Without even a quick summation of her worldly possessions Carolyn knew she didn't have a single item she wouldn't trade to share in that ignorance again.

She stepped out of her car, opened the trunk, and retrieved the flag she'd put there for safekeeping. For the seven-hour drive home the folded cloth lay rested in her lap.

The corners of Carolyn's mouth formed a rigid grimace and

her left eye twitched with an involuntary jerk as the miles slipped by in a miserable, yet otherwise uneventful drone. But for remembering to unclench her teeth to relieve her massive headache, her mind was numb.

The desire to run from everything she'd known and loved, her refurbished old house, her successful construction company, and her few close friends, began when she arrived home.

A small, unassuming brown package lay tossed against her screen door. As she bent for closer inspection, she recognized the flourished M of her brother's first name on the return-address label. Carolyn's face grew ashen and pale as her spine slumped round like a bag full of rags.

"What?" she whispered in disbelief.

Her hands trembled and her legs buckled as her purse and suitcase slid to her feet. Her grip on the flag tightened for a moment before it also tumbled to the sidewalk. Tiny pricks from the nubby sisal doormat burned her knees as she knelt and fumbled with the package.

A large golden A above Aydin's Jewelry decorated the dainty box. Between the tissue paper, smelling of far-away dusty antique shops and cigarette smoke, was a gold-and-diamond ankle chain with an engraved heart clasp. Carolyn stared at the precious metal and delicate gems cradled in the hollow of her hand. They flashed in the sunlight in poignant opposition to the gloom and shadow that were every part of her life now. She searched through the thin paper, the odor reminding her of camels, heavy kilims, and blazing sunsets–her brother's world.

No note. Only an inscription on the clasp: Open your heart ~ Look within.

It took a moment before she realized he must have sent it before he died. He'd always told her she had an inner strength. How fitting that he would remind her when she needed it the most. But how would he have known she'd need to hear this now? Her fingers trembled as she struggled to slide the exquisite chain around her ankle. She stood as a bitter rage came over her.

"No!" she cried, drawing out the last of the word in anguish.

Carolyn realized she was blessed in many ways. But she'd suffered a few harsh blows long before this. Until now, she'd thought adversity made you work harder, try harder, and give more of yourself.

There would be a reward for effort. Isn't that what we're always taught? You're given extra points for persevering in rough times, putting up with hardships, tolerating and forgiving ill treatment. There would be a prize at the end. Love, joy, and happiness.

Right?

"Wrong!" she spewed.

The anger and resentment boiled higher as she realized it'd all been a lie.

"A damn lie!" she hissed.

Carolyn's once loved home, contented and cheerful, where she'd laughed with her mother and brother at the absurdity of the old days stood holding only painful memories. It was a cold, empty vault primed with eagerness to consume her with sorrow.

It had all been too much and she needed to get away. Away from her big prize, her wondrous reward. Her mind pinged between defiance and the fear of being lost forever in this misery.

Carolyn shook. From anger or the vain attempt to gather the fragmented shards of herself, she wasn't sure. But she forced her hand steady as she rustled in her purse to find the house keys. The merry ringtone she'd paid four dollars for and an hour to find chimed out causing her to jump.

She jammed the decline button as she unlocked the door, partly to silence the now annoying tune but also, she wasn't ready to talk to anyone.

In a dark corner of her closet she pushed aside a stack of sweaters and set down the flag. She knelt in silence gripping its edges for a long time. Before leaving the room she piled the sweaters on top. She didn't know why. She knew she couldn't bury her loss.

On her way back out to her car, she felt the weight of the chain dangling around her narrow ankle. It gave her a small measure of her brother's presence. It was more comfort than she'd known since she'd heard the news. She tossed her suitcase and purse in the back seat.

Carolyn's mind raced somewhere reckless and untamed—an unfamiliar place until now. And without hesitation, she followed. If she kept moving, the grief and memory would billow behind her, like the exhaust from an old, beat-up muscle car.

Carolyn didn't want to remember. Memories were painful. Being here was agonizing. So she pressed hard on the gas pedal and raced away.

On and on she drove, faster and farther, hoping time would reverse if only she were quick enough. The perfect white rose lay with honor and dignity in the seat next to her where, despite blurring past speed limit signs, it perished a few brief hours after attaining its most magnificent moment.

Her brother's death had been the beginning of it. It had changed everything. In her thirty-three years of living on this earth, this had been her most despised day.

She hadn't realized it at the time, but living beyond that day would become almost as difficult.

CAROL GOODNIGHT

CHAPTER 2

Carolyn's wide, vacant eyes focused on an imaginary point in the darkness as she sped along the pitted blacktop. On impulse she veered into the right lane and took the exit heading south. Once back in the fast lane, her mind wandered. She remembered despite herself.

Magical summer evenings, cool fresh cut grass, finding animals, dragons, and castles in the clouds filled the empty road ahead of her. She remembered how she and her brother would imagine an entire global sail while tying together a few odd logs to make a raft on the creek behind the house. When they'd found an old lawn mower engine down at the dump, they tinkered and pulled it apart, all the while imagining they would follow the Grand Prix route over various countries when they grew up, always winning, always together. She never thought it strange to get lost in imagination.

I guess I always thought we'd get around to those things, she thought as her dreams for the life she and her brother planned disintegrated behind her at ninety-two miles an hour.

Pale moonlight spilled over the highway lessening the darkness as Carolyn forged a path through the impenetrable maze of her loss. The flicker of scudding clouds tempted to lull her into a false sense of security.

She glanced into the night sky. Witchy Pitchfork!

The moon witch glared at her. She looked angry as if she were resentful she to be up on a night like this.

"Damn witch!" Carolyn said under her breath as she remembered.

After many nights of moon gazing, she and her brother agreed that the light and dark shapes on the moon's surface resembled a witch holding a pitchfork. They checked and confirmed it to each other often over the years.

"Witchy Pitchfork!" they would say, sometimes in unison.

Carolyn pulled down the visor.

"Damn that old witch." She blinked back tears.

The quiet drone of the road hummed until she opened the window for air. The gust blew her auburn hair in every direction as the sweet fragrance of meadow grasses mixed with the resinous asphalt.

Summer nights, she remembered.

Their mother was a kind, sweet woman, and they both adored her. But there was a foreboding presence in their life. The stepfather. They'd grown up in a large old farmhouse under the oppressive control of the stepfather. The man had no love for them, nor did he ever feign it for their mother's sake. She'd been a beautiful woman, running from their alcoholic father, whom she'd divorced before she met the stepfather. He came on strong. She fell for it. They married and the hell began.

As early as five, Mike would pat her back with his little chubby hand when they'd hear his footsteps enter the house. They knew to cower and hide from his pinched expressions and narrowing eyes as he filled their lives with his thick contempt. While he was sometimes fine, even jovial and charming, they'd learned to never let their guard down as he could change in a split second.

Their mother became afraid of him herself and often begged them to avoid disturbing him in any way. They all lived with the same general sense of dread.

She and her brother learned to look out for each other as they played, fought, and laughed. Laughing, as it turned out, was one of the worst crimes. Even smiling, for that matter.

"What are you so damned happy about?" he would ask if he caught them smiling.

The answer, "Nothing," only brought a barrage of name calling and threats of a trip to the home where other unfortunate children smiled at nothing.

That was particularly hard for Mike, she remembered. He had an inner joy that was hard to squelch. He got a kick out of everything, it seemed.

But they figured out soon enough that when they were rarely caught smiling they would say they were remembering what some stupid kid at school had done. That seemed to satisfy him somewhat. They could almost hear him thinking about the idiot kid at school surrounded by bullies laughing at him. Yeah, he liked that thought, all right. None of that had ever happened, but they had stories ready in case he asked for details. Smiling was a lot of work back then.

The road droned on as her memory lingered in the past.

The thing that frightened her the most, she remembered, was when he'd end his rants with, "One of these days I will murder all of you people."

She came to appreciate the distinction of "you people", meaning he didn't include himself in their ilk.

In the dark with the blanket pulled over her head, she'd listen to the century-old oak tree scratching at her window and worry about his threats.

What would she do if he went into a murderous rampage one night and killed them? Or sometimes she'd worry about Raw Head and Bloody Bones, the two hideous monsters he'd told them lived in the attic above her room. She'd never seen them of course, but she imagined what they looked like. The rustling creaks and groans of the old house disguised the sound of them up there, creeping and crawling, plotting and planning. As a child, she thought they were afraid of the stepfather too, which is why she never actually saw them.

Lying awake, listening to night sounds was the beginning of her insomnia and hypervigilance.

"Was that a sound? Where did it come from?" she'd ask as she lay silent and held her breath to listen. Sometimes when she was particularly scared, maybe the stepfather had had a bad day at work, or any number of the vast possibilities that set him off, she would sneak down from her bedroom and hide. Squeezed between the cheap paneled wall and the scratchy green fabric of the couch, she tried to make herself as small as possible. She slept little on those nights.

The stepfather worked on that old house, but he wasn't a very good carpenter. When her mother would suggest a better way to do a project he would scowl. Who knew what punishment she suffered for those perceived insults?

Carolyn and her brother, otherwise known as Useless and Worthless, sat with him for hours while he worked on his projects. They were responsible for handing him his tools much as a surgeon has his scalpel handed to him. God help them if they handed him the wrong tool.

"Hey Useless, hand me the Phillip's head. That's not a damn Philip's head," he would say, and off it flew across the room.

One of them would scamper to get it before he needed it while trying not to do anything that would draw attention or set him off again.

She was thankful that he put a roof over her head. But even as a child she knew life didn't need to be so shitty.

After leaving home at eighteen, and a brief marriage, which

was nothing more than changing one bad situation with another, she bought an old rundown house. All those years of watching and helping with projects had given her an instinct and common knowledge of how things went together.

The neighbors watched as she whipped her place into shape. After seeing what she could do, they would call on her when they needed help or advice. Before long, she quit her receptionist job and started a handy-gal service. She studied in the evenings for her contractor's license, and as time went on, she grew successful with her own construction company. She'd fought going into construction for years until that one day she realized it came naturally to her. Being shy, it wasn't easy at first to sell herself in business. But as she grew more confident, word of her good work and fair prices spread.

So there! she'd think every time her stepfather came into her mind.

Her brother followed her a month later, at fifteen, after a brawl he'd finally won.

Carolyn choked back a sob as she remembered Mike telling her of how he had held the stepfather to the dirt.

With tears in his eyes, he told her, "I yelled at him - I'm supposed to love you, not beat the shit out of you. I let go of his shirt and left," he'd said.

Carolyn helped him with money all she could in those days, but she was still in the middle of a rough marriage at the time. Mike moved in with a friend and his family from school. They welcomed him and let him work at their family gas station for room and board until he graduated from high school. He then walked straight down to the recruiter's office and joined the Air Force. His first choice of military occupational specialty was the military police. On weekends and evenings he took advantage of the education program and attained a degree in international relations, minoring in criminal justice. After his stint in the Air Force, he'd applied to the CIA and was given a place in the professional trainee program. He worked as an operations desk officer until his dedication and hard work got him an invitation into the Clandestine Service Trainee program.

Carolyn had been so proud of him. In only a few short years, he'd become a Special Agent.

It had made sense he was CIA, she'd thought. What fear would a man have of anyone if he'd been threatened with murder from the time he was three years old? Not much, she realized.

That hideous day of the phone call came to Carolyn's mind. Not sure how she'd gotten there, she'd found herself on the carpet. An agonized voice coming from some unknown hell kept screaming the word "*NO!*"

Somehow, she wasn't there any longer but that gut-wrenching sound wouldn't stop. It hadn't mattered how much she wailed and choked and cried though.

He was gone.

Perhaps because of the bond they'd formed, they'd made plans for a future that included the other. They'd survived the grim childhood and were starting to enjoy the wonderful things they'd planned while they'd gazed at the clouds and moon.

That's gone now.

Carolyn turned up the radio. She didn't like being alone with her thoughts. There had to be sound. Always. Ever since she'd been a child in that old farmhouse she'd needed background noise to distract her from the creaks and groans that rambled through her mind.

Now that Mike was gone, it was worse.

Every night since he'd passed away, she'd lain in the dark and sobbed to exhaustion. But it hadn't mattered. Not a single tear.

He was gone.

At the first stop to get fuel she called her foreman.

"Fernando. Finish the high-rise project we're working on and then bid out work under my license. It's time for you to get ready for your own business. This will be an opportunity for you to test the waters, big guy," she said, glad to help him take the next step.

As she hung up, Carolyn pulled on her sunglasses, gunned the engine, and drove the next six and a half hours as fast as she possibly could.

Miles of blurred landscape zipped by under the full throttle of her steady hand. She gripped the wheel and sped by other motorists feeling as if she were the lead during a qualifying lap. All the while she knew she would never, and could never, win the race she was running. In fact, she felt as if she were teetering on the edge of losing it all.

On the verge of collapse, she pulled over to get a room for the night. The irritating lights that had followed her for the last hour pulled off the exit too. The driver wheeled into the same hotel parking lot but sat in his car as she walked in to register. She looked over at him. His car was a 1960's gold color. Ugly.

Must be grabbing a last smoke. I bet that car stinks!

A red glow from the driver's cigarette tip flickered as he took a drag. He turned his face away from her and exhaled a hazy grey ghost that swirled through the thick murk until it melded with his cloud of smog.

Weird, the things that come into your mind.

The Tennessee Valley Authority hotel she'd chosen sat nestled into the hillside next to the enormous dam. The girl behind the desk handed her the room key.

"This room has a nice view over the water, ma'am. You'll love it," she said.

Carolyn hoped her wince at the girl's cheerfulness didn't register on her face.

"Thank you," she said.

With a growing numbness, she rolled her suitcase to the elevator and pressed the button to the third floor.

"Room 307?" she asked herself, as if searching to find meaning in the words. There was no meaning. It was only a room number she realized as she trudged down the hall.

"Man! I'm tired," she said.

Dust particles clouded around her as she flopped on the bed. She pulled the blanket back to get a pillow when the shimmering diamonds and gold around her ankle caught her eye.

I'll never see my brother again.

These last few days Carolyn had survived by running full-force until she crashed in an effort to escape the nightmare.

As her thoughts stilled, a muddled dream floated through her subconscious. A faint echo of the sweet baby words of her brother reverberated through the darkness of time.

"Tiss do night."

He'd said it every evening after their mother shouted "kiss goodnight," from downstairs to let them know it was time to settle down. It was her earliest and fondest memory of them both.

"Kiss goodnight, brother," she said.

Exhaustion ebbed her to the brink of consciousness where it lingered before dragging her to the oblivion of sleep.

As another empty morning dawned, sunlight crept through the open curtains. Hideous green walls and a stale musty odor welcomed her to another senseless day.

She'd forgotten where she was. She'd forgotten her brother had died. A panic gripped her. Nothing was familiar. Then she remembered.

"I'm nowhere," she whispered.

CAROL GOODNIGHT

CHAPTER 3

A little over a week later Carolyn found herself sitting with her convertible top down at a traffic light on Decatur Street in the French Quarter.

To her right, the busy waiters in old-fashioned soda jerk hats and bow ties trailed powdered sugar while bobbing and weaving enormous trays of chicory coffee and fluffy beignets through the crowd at the Café Du Monde.

It was just after lunch on that fateful, steamy afternoon that a shiny white Bentley rolled up next to her. On the fringes of her primal awareness, Carolyn could sense someone staring at her. She glanced over her shoulder to the left. The handsome driver nodded. Carolyn nodded in return.

Not at all sure why, she found herself smiling. In truth, it was not a smile at all, but less of the frown that she'd become accustomed to this last week.

That evening she sat sipping a Bloody Mary in the tropical courtyard garden of her hotel, only a few steps, but worlds away from the famous Bourbon Street.

Banana trees and tall flowering ginger shaded the sitting areas making each table feel partially enclosed and private. Lavender wisteria and coral bougainvillea spilled gracefully over the old brickwork surrounding the garden. A mass profusion of colorful canna and bromeliads circled the gurgling fountain in the center of the courtyard while fragrant sweet olive trees almost reached the balconies that overlooked the grounds.

Carolyn thumbed through a small pocket-size history booklet of New Orleans she'd found at a stall in the French Market. It explained that in early Colonial days the old French-influenced properties of the Quarter were wide and spacious with the houses sitting in the middle of the lot. The kitchen gardens spread around the outside.

But after the two great fires in the late eighteenth century, residents built houses closer together on deeper and narrower lots. Buildings had common sidewalls, and the street fronts were continuous. This led to open spaces behind the property that gave rise to walled courtyards.

After the Civil War, the beautiful landscaped gardens were harder to find. The immigrant poor used the former lush gardens for bathing, raising chickens and outdoor kitchens.

Old photograph collections she'd seen in one of the antique shops on Royal Street pictured houses with peeling paint, tottering outdoor stairways, and small plots with no vegetation. In the 1920's, a long overdue renaissance gathered steam when architecture-loving residents in the historic district founded the Vieux Carré Commission.

Carolyn sat staring at the bougainvillea-covered brick wall, deep in thought. As she popped an olive in her mouth, she imagined the children who might have played here one hundred years ago.

Her Bloody Mary consisted of celery, of course, three olives, a large bacon wrapped shrimp, and a small block of pepper jack cheese. A pickled bean and a pod of okra dangled out the side of the tall, house-brand Cajun spice rimmed glass. If she finished this she wouldn't need dinner, she'd decided.

A handsome, well-dressed man, whom she recognized from

the traffic light earlier that afternoon walked past. He smiled as if he may have recognized her as well.

His smile, gleaming bright with the perfect teeth of a model, unnerved her as he turned back and leaned in toward her. Electric-shock blue eyes, like two glittering cubes of arctic ice, gazed at her from his strong square face and high cheekbones. The combination of his Grecian nose and sculpted face resulted in a classically handsome man.

He was tall, about six foot one, she guessed, and he towered over her with a nonchalant yet self-confident air as he leaned in closer.

When he held out his hand, she extended hers in return. He grasped only her fingertips.

"Hello. My name is Andrew. And who might you be?"

Carolyn's heart skipped a bit of a beat.

She responded with only "Carolyn", unable to think of anything witty to say. He brought her fingertips to his lips and kissed them.

Her heart skipped the rest of the beat

"Now I remember where I've seen you," he said while shaking his finger back and forth with a smile.

His voice, relaxed with a soft timbre, instilled in her an immediate feeling of ease.

"You were the beauty driving the black Thunderbird in front of The Cafe Dumonde."

Carolyn gave him a timid smile and lowered her face. Her cheeks burned.

"Yes, yes, that *was* you," he said with a broad smile.

"May I help you?" asked the waitress.

"Oh, I'm sorry. I'm in the way. I'm pestering this beautiful young lady. Don't mind me," Andrew said as he bent forward and bowed his head. He gave the waitress a bashful smile before turning his head and winking at Carolyn.

Carolyn opened her mouth to speak, but nothing came. After

a silent pause with Andrew still smiling at her, she smiled back at him.

"May I invite myself to share your table?" he asked. "All the others are taken."

Carolyn glanced around the courtyard and realized that the tables were all full.

"Sure," she said, feeling more at ease.

Oh, he only wants to share a table.

She smiled at her silly imagination.

And so… the story of Andrew begins.

At that first meeting, he was charming, wonderful, and funny. And so handsome.

He'd entertained her for close to an hour with tales of his family heritage and his many successful corporations before making his apologies and excusing himself. If it had been any other man, he would have said goodbye and left. Andrew was different. He was grand and theatrical. He was confident and self-assured. He was unlike anyone she'd ever met.

As she watched him walk away, he turned and looked back. He smiled, and while his gaze was soft, his eyes lingered on her longer than was comfortable.

While usually stoic, the blush on Carolyn's cheeks threatened to sear through her face. Suddenly feeling awkward again, she looked down and fumbled with the limp celery stalk in her empty cocktail glass. She'd dated little in high school, and since leaving her husband two years ago, she'd had little interest in finding another man problem. She'd gotten along fine with her crew, but that was a different type of relationship altogether.

When she looked back, Andrew was gone.

CAROL GOODNIGHT

CHAPTER 4

Two days later Carolyn lay in bed with her eyes open. The room was dark but for the muted glow of dawn peeking through the blinds.

Another day. She groaned before reaching over and turning on the bedside lamp.

Her elbow knocked a stack of brochures to the floor. As she leaned to retrieve them, she noticed a large green dragon on the top one. She picked them up and walked toward the window to open the blinds. A ghost-gray mist trailed through the street below. It blurred the garish marquis, the spirits-gift-luggage store, and the numerous restaurants across Canal St. to resemble a lovely old painting.

She set the brochures on the counter and prepared a cup of coffee in the tiny one-cup coffee pot. As she waited, the dragon caught her eye again. The colorful papier-mâché' and sculpted-foam Mardi Gras float beckoned her with a mischievous smile. So, she decided rather than lay in bed all day, as she had the day before, she'd go to a behind-the-scene tour of Mardi Gras World.

She rifled through the stack of brochures. She knew the museums would fill empty time with distraction.

Love a good museum. Fills gaps. The words from the movie *Rocky* came to her with a new meaning as she sighed.

Before heading out, she dressed and answered all the texts

she'd received the two previous days.

She wrote two sets of replies, one to her business associates and one to those sending condolences.

With that accomplished, she realized she was completely free. No responsibilities, no problems to solve, no one asking questions about her brother's death that she couldn't bear to answer.

Free! She pulled the door closed behind her.

The doorman swung open the lobby door as Carolyn approached. She zipped her jacket as she stepped through the double doors.

"Thank you," she said with a shiver.

"It'll burn off soon enough," said the doorman. "The clouds are lazy this mornin'. They'd rather take it easy down here with us than hang up in the sky where they belong. That's New Orleans for ya."

Carolyn forced a smile.

"Have a nice day," she said.

She sighed as she turned toward the parking garage and wondered if she'd ever feel truly happy again.

Lush palms lined the center of Canal St. where a noisy streetcar rumbled past the yellow glow of street-lamps in a two-dimensional silhouette of dark grey. Soot-coated trash cans and construction dumpsters appeared soft and delicate in the haze while the higher buildings disappeared altogether in a swirl of white.

A hollow muffle from Carolyn's footsteps echoed on the granite sidewalk. She turned to see if anyone was following her.

"For crying out loud!" she said, not sure where her nervousness was coming from. This was a city. There were people here. People walked on the sidewalks.

She couldn't put her finger on it, but she'd had an odd feeling the last few days. Mike would have called it hinky, but she just thought of it as the creeps.

She wondered if maybe she should've stayed home. But the

minute she remembered being back there with the memories, she shook her head.

Once behind the wheel of her car, she stared at herself in the rearview mirror.

Mike wouldn't want her to be so glum. He traveled and enjoyed life. He'd be pissed if he knew she was feeling this way.

He'd always asked to go with him on ski trips and Mediterranean cruises when he had free time.

She'd always meant to.

From the mirror she saw a large, hulking figure approaching her car. His long, awkward strides caused her heartbeat to quicken.

Were there other people here?

Lost in her own fog, she hadn't noticed. She turned around and realized she was alone in the dark garage. A shock sparked through her as she clicked the door lock. Her eyes widened as she looked back to see the man still moving toward her. There was something familiar about his hunched forward gait.

She held her breath.

The huge bald man crouched behind her car and looked at her reflection in her mirror. The pasty white skin on his large, square forehead wrinkled as his dark eyes squinted at her. His face was expressionless. Carolyn sat frozen.

I have pepper spray!

But before she could remember where it was, the man stood up, pulled his phone from his pocket, and walked away.

Carolyn drew in a breath.

"Where is that damn pepper spray?" she asked as she rustled through the glove compartment.

When she found it, she crammed it in her purse.

She sat for a moment before remembering she'd been trying to give herself a pep talk.

"OK. Now get on with it!" she told herself.

After a few wrong turns, she found herself greeted into the

parking lot of Mardi Gras World by a giant reproduction alligator.

"Mardi Gras Warehouse is more like it," she mumbled.

She found a close spot in the near-empty parking lot behind the concrete barrier that separated the train tracks and industrial riverfront area from the rest of the city.

To the left, the double expanses of the Crescent City Connection loomed overhead. It stretched across the winding Mississippi river beyond the warehouse.

The hair on her arms prickled as she looked up at the bridge.

There was that hinky feeling again. She hated bridges.

She decided right then to stay on this side of the city.

Weird though, they'd never given her the creeps before. Nervousness, yes, but never the creeps.

A gold, purple and green jester head as big as a car held its hand in a permanent wave as she passed through to the entrance.

Traces of sun glowed through the fog as she stepped into the enormous building. From the inside it looked even larger. The huge entrance area divided into paths that led in several directions.

"Sorry, ma'am. The guide's runnin' late this morning," said the guy unloading boxes at the entrance. "Something about his kid. Want to wait? Or go by yourself?"

The stuffy corridors lay expectant, waiting for an audience to show-off their colorful magic.

"I'm fine by myself," Carolyn answered as she took off her jacket.

Everywhere she looked, vibrant smiling faces grinned at her. She couldn't help but compare them to a candy store or a fantastical bakery displaying giant cakes. They reminded her she'd forgotten to eat breakfast.

Long twisting corridors crammed full with woodland nymphs, super heroes, all manner of sea creatures, and flowers, towered over her. Some were so high they reached into the rafters.

Carolyn wandered a good half an hour before she spotted a

chandelier. It hung like a dazzle of armpit hair under the arm of a ten-foot-tall Fred Flintstone.

Curious as to how they'd attached it to the float, she wound her way toward it through the endless trail. She leaned over a dusty Alice in Wonderland caterpillar to get a better look. At a distance, the light on the crystals looked like precious gems, but she could see they were only cut glass.

As she pulled back, her blouse caught on the caterpillar's hookah. When she leaned forward to untangle it, she caught a slight movement out of the corner of her eye.

What was that?

She stood still while her eyes darted through the display pieces. After a full minute of standing frozen, she heard a group of tourists heading in her direction.

That's enough! she thought, wondering if she should've stayed in bed.

She took a step toward the exit when a brown blur of fur bee-lined straight at her feet.

Carolyn screamed.

The rat jerked to a stop under the dangling beard of a gruesome swamp creature. It wiggled its whiskers and sniffed the air before it took off in a zig-zag between the cluttered props.

"Everything all right back there, ma'am?" one of the employees called out.

"A rat!" she shouted as she hurried back toward the entrance.

"Yeah. We try to keep 'em out. Some of the cats are even scared of 'em." He laughed.

The parking lot was beginning to fill up when she reached her car. As she buckled her seatbelt, she thought about the movement. It couldn't have been a rat. It was shoulder high. She sat still for a moment trying to piece her thoughts together. Something seemed off.

She shook her head. "Well, rats climb," she said as her stomach rumbled in hunger. Her eyebrows furrowed as she pulled on her sunglasses and tried to remember where she'd seen the sign for crab-cake benedicts.

CHAPTER 5

Later that afternoon, Carolyn walked to the Café' Dumonde for a cup of chicory coffee. She crossed back over the street and walked through Jackson square sipping the piping hot liquid through the tiny swizzle hole. The fog had burned off and the air was hot and muggy, but she knew if she didn't have a little caffeine she'd be in bed by seven again.

A group of teenage boys playing a lively jazz tune drew her their way. Carolyn took a seat on a bench in the shade of the St. Louis Cathedral to listen.

As the hour turned four, a rich peal of bells clanged from the bell tower of the church. The out of pitch notes blended with the circus-like atmosphere and off-beat pulse gathered below. The jazz group finished their number and waited on the bells as they discussed their next tune.

Carolyn was watching a fortune teller try to entice a tourist into her chair when she saw Andrew turn the corner and head her way. She felt excited to see him, but also a little anxious.

She was sure he wouldn't remember her. Why would he? He must know beautiful women all over the world.

As he came closer, she closed her eyes and took a deep breath. After her recent loss, her confidence was at its lowest and she'd cared little about anything. Especially handsome strangers.

Out of the corner of her eye, she watched as he walked straight toward her. She picked at the plastic lid of her coffee cup and tried to appear nonchalant.

"Well, hello there," Andrew said.

Carolyn looked up and tried to act surprised.

"Oh. Hi."

"Carolyn, right?" he asked.

Before she answered, he went on, "How are you this lovely day?"

"I'm fine. It is a lovely day," she responded.

If she'd known him better, the first thing she would've told him would've been about the incident in the warehouse. Had he been her brother, they would've thoroughly discussed the matter by now. They'd have imagined every possible scenario before he would end by telling her he had work to do and it was nothing more than her vivid imagination.

"Gotta go, sis. Love ya," She remembered his sign-off.

She turned toward Andrew before the memory could jab her further.

After a few more pleasantries about the weather, Andrew asked if he could sit with her.

"Oh, of course," she said as she slid over a smidge.

"So what brings you to New Orleans? Alcohol, voodoo, or the food?" Andrew asked.

Carolyn laughed. She couldn't tell him what brought her here. She hadn't yet found the words to describe it. So she listened to him talk about his latest adventure in South America.

"I refurbished an old, rusted out factory along the Amazon and started manufacturing for export. I'm making a killing so far."

"What are you manufacturing?" she asked.

Andrew paused for a moment. "That rust in the jungle is a killer!" He laughed. "You put up any kind of metal and it's rusted the next day."

As Andrew avoided her question, Carolyn was reminded of Sandy, the braggadocious girl who had moved next door when they were in junior high. She'd been an expert in diverting questions.

As Andrew continued talking about the jungle, Carolyn's mind drifted to the summer-long monopoly games she'd played with her brother and Sandy. Her eyes went glassy as she stared at the church and remembered that every fall, right before school would begin, Sandy would find a way to cheat them. After the second summer, they refused to play with her.

Andrew pulled out his phone. She turned back to him with a start. She hadn't realized she'd let her mind wander.

The last thing she remembered him saying was something about a village and giving children shoes. He held up the screen and Carolyn saw a picture of him standing in the middle of twenty-five or thirty smiling kids, all wearing orange crocs.

"Aw. How precious," she said.

Andrew reached his hand to block the screen in the sun, and in the process caressed Carolyn's hand. She looked down at his hand touching hers. It was a casual gesture, nothing more. But she felt a small intimacy growing between that put her more at ease.

They sat in silence a few minutes listening to the band play another song. When they'd finished, Andrew asked if he could see her in the late afternoon of the following day. She agreed to meet him in her hotel courtyard where they'd first met.

"I'd like to take you on a tour of one of the historic cemeteries nearby. You'll love it," he said.

Carolyn didn't mention her brother's death. And while it felt too soon to sight-see at a graveyard, she'd always wanted to see the above-ground cemeteries. So she didn't balk at Andrew's invitation.

As she watched the sun catch the highlights in his blond hair, she tried to convince herself it would be fine. She rarely dated, especially so soon after meeting someone.

But it was an afternoon date, she reasoned as she realized that since her brother's death, the old rules and timeline of her life had shifted.

She found herself smiling again. This time the corners of her mouth turned up.

CAROL GOODNIGHT

CHAPTER 6

It was evening when they arrived at the cemetery, despite meeting in the late afternoon. Andrew had insisted they have a long, lovely lunch. Afterward he'd made a stop to run an errand that left her waiting in his car, alone, for about twenty minutes. The sight of tourists on the narrow street where he'd illegally parked kept her entertained. But before long, she found her impatience rising along with the heat. She began to visualize the route back to her hotel.

She'd removed her hat, wiped her brow, and thought how rude he was when Andrew came bounding around the corner. He apologized profusely and said he had planned a special surprise for her.

Carolyn's brows furrowed in as she looked at him in confusion.

Andrew laughed. "Trust me, kiddo. It'll be good."

Kiddo. She rather liked the sound of that.

In spite of the skeptical start, all of his attention was on her as they strolled through the cemetery grounds. Andrew held an umbrella by his side and used it somewhat as a cane as he walked with a nice straight posture.

Carolyn thought he looked rather distinguished as she pulled open the map.

"We don't need that," he said. "I've studied this place."

Carolyn looked up at him.

Handsome and smart.

"New Orleans cemeteries are much like New Orleans itself," he began.

"Destitute in some areas and opulent in others. Both with equal flair and style. Legend has it that a certain Charles Howard, having been refused membership into the Metairie Jockey Club because he was not an aristocrat, vowed to get even with the snobbish blue bloods."

"Personally, I rather like snobbish blue bloods," he laughed.

"Anyway, he declared that one day their exclusive playground would be his. He planned to turn it into an eternal resting place for everyone. After the Civil War, he took his opportunity for revenge."

Andrew paused, stood looking in the sky, and laughed as if he'd told a personal joke.

Carolyn wondered what was so funny, thinking she must have missed something.

"You see, the Jockey Club had fallen on hard times due to mismanagement, and it was at this opportune moment that Mr. Howard set about with his plan. I can relate," he added.

"He constructed his own spectacular tomb on the exact spot of the former Jockey clubhouse and surrounded it with the cemetery, still in the oval of a racetrack. In this city of the dead, they built the elaborate stone crypts and mausoleums above the muddy, black gumbo soil so the loved ones don't slide away in the all-too-often rain that raises the high water table even higher."

Carolyn's eyes widened at the thought.

"Row after row of these amazing architectural tombs of marble, bronze, and sometimes decorated with stained glass, line up similar to a neighborhood. Even in death, the wealthy try to keep up with the Joneses."

After he finished his rehearsed spiel, he was quiet.

CAROL GOODNIGHT

"Were you a tour guide here, Andrew? You seem to know quite a bit about this cemetery."

"Just a hobby," he responded. "Love a grave yard."

The mist rose higher as they strolled deeper into the cemetery. Overcast skies dimmed in the early evening light. The clouds, which usually conjured thoughts of cheerfulness when puffy and white, felt like ghostly souls as they drifted over the graves.

Carolyn's thoughts drifted as well. She imagined a spirit world where the ghosts congregated and looked down at their mini mansions or their barely afforded wooden markers.

The once-gleaming imperishable marble angels were eroding and imprisoned with a mossy patina of verdigris.

Creeping ivy wound through the overgrown lichen to give the oldest of them the look of a hunched topiary. Tree roots twining around the neck and torso of one sweet-faced cherub, like skeleton claws with a grisly choke-hold, sent a shudder up Carolyn's spine. She looked away.

Banana trees and other tropical plants that had struggled time and again to establish themselves before the caretaker plucked them or gave them a zap with his weed eater were once again emerging triumphantly from the rich alluvial soil. In contrast, a single strand of purple beads and a frayed and faded golden ribbon hung over an ornate wrought iron fence as a sad, gaudy New Orleans style memento.

Without warning, a gust of wind rustled through the live oak trees. Branches swayed and brittle dead leaves chased pell-mell through the aging vaults and monuments playing tag with ancient sentiments. The deepening amethyst shadows at the edge of the cemetery crept toward Carolyn and Andrew, embracing them in the splendid purple shawl of evening.

Through this light, this twilight, this thin rising vapor during the afterglow of day, only a mere wisp separates us from our loved ones.

Sometimes, like now, dusk, she felt her brother very close.

If only I could reach…
They walked on.

Black-bordered crosses with grief-scrawled names rested like whispers under drooping willows and mossy oaks. Behind them, the mightiest marble statues proclaimed their passion with silent, lifeless faces and soulless stares. A hush descended on the cemetery as fingers of night reached one by one through the old rusty ironwork, bleached marble tombs, and empty-eyed stone statues. Each departed resident had lived a life, had a story that could only be wondered about - the only clue - a vague headstone. An entire life summarized in a word or two.

As they walked to the back of the cemetery, the clouds broke at the horizon. A small beam of sunshine cut through the overcast sky and pierced through a mausoleum window. A blue light glowing from inside caused Andrew to open the heavy door and peer in. Seeing only an angel statue, he held the door for Carolyn to step in first. As Carolyn got closer to the somber blue light, an odd feeling crept over her.

A blue stained-glass window set to the west caught the last rays of the setting sun. A single shaft of light shimmered through the darkness and spread a haunting, smooth glow over the angel and her ward.

Carolyn shook, and a quick gasp caught in her throat.

As she edged closer, she could see the life-size angel draped over a crypt. The stone face, bowed in grief, slumped still on her hand. Her other hand hung in front of her, resting limply and forever in nothingness. Her massive wings reached up over her shoulders, shrouding her head, and then drooped down the length of the tomb where the tips then rested on the floor.

The angel languished over the tomb, one knee bent with her toes touching the step. The other leg stretched out behind her, lay flat under her flowing gown, as if she'd collapsed there in her despondency.

CAROL GOODNIGHT

Carolyn staggered backward, her mind swirling with her own sense of loss. The tiny mausoleum spun in a haze. Andrew was next to her in a moment and caught her before she fell. He searched her face. Her dilated pupils could be seen through the slits of her almost closed eyes. He swung his arm under her legs, lifted her, and carried her through the now completely dark graveyard.

A brisk gust of wind murmured through the canopy of leaves and dangling Spanish moss before groaning low along the hallowed ground, and then race through the desolate tombs with a piteous moan.

The clouds circled above in sinister swirls as the air temperature dropped. Dead leaves blew so high that Andrew lowered his face into Carolyn's to keep the debris from his eyes as she uttered an agonizing sound. His step caught for a moment before he continued on.

They were almost at the cemetery parking lot when she woke. Feeling embarrassed but still shaky, she didn't argue with him when he insisted on carrying her the rest of the way to his car. He winced as his knee dug into the gravel when he bent to set her down.

"You gave me quite a scare," he said.

"I have no idea why that happened. I'm so sorry."

Andrew stared at her, frozen and unblinking, before a soft expression returned to his eyes. He tilted his face back and looked down on her with a pensive smile as he touched her cheek with the side of his thumb. As he leaned forward, his warm breath traced the slender nape of her neck until his lips tickled her ear.

Carolyn's face flushed.

Andrew glided his hands down the length of her arms until she could feel the heat of his palms pressed against her fingertips. She sat frozen. Andrew hesitated for a moment, smiled, and then entwined his fingers around hers. He continued kneeling in the gravel next to her as she wondered if he could feel the beat of her heart.

Finally, she took a deep breath.

"I'm feeling much better. The air was so stuffy in the

mausoleum. I'm much better now, really. Thank you," she said, the words tumbling out of her mouth.

Andrew reached behind her, and before she realized it, his arms were tight around her waist with his fingers pulling at her back. She found herself sinking, yielding into his yearning grasp with a helpless surrender. The fresh scent of lemons lingered on his smooth, clenching jaw as his face brushed her cheek. She closed her eyes as his eager, insistent lips pressed against her mouth. The world fell away behind them, and her mind became fuzzy and withdrew from the harsh place it had been residing as she found herself faint and kissing Andrew in return.

CAROL GOODNIGHT

CHAPTER 7

A beautiful bouquet of red camellias arrived at Carolyn's hotel room that evening while she readied herself for a dinner date with Andrew. She'd never been the recipient of such attention before, and she hated to admit it, but she found it exhilarating.

Andrew knocked on the door shortly after the flowers arrived. As he stepped in, he took her hand and pulled her body close to his. Squeezing one arm around her waist, he kissed the tip of her perfect bow-shaped lips. Before she could pull away, he nuzzled a trail down her neck. Tiny goose bumps rose on the back of her arms as he took her hand and led her out the door. The ever-present sadness of her loss lifted as she wondered what her brother would think of this royal treatment. He'd tease her for sure.

With a smile, she crooked her arm in Andrew's as they ventured out into the Quarter for a long stroll amongst sweet-smelling confederate jasmine, fried green tomatoes, and large pots of pungent boiling crawfish.

The sumptuous dinner crawl to many of New Orleans' finest restaurants would last for hours.

The evening began on Bourbon Street with an absinthe cocktail in a dark, historic, cave-like café, once the sight of a Spanish colonial prison. The atmosphere was dark and dingy in the low-ceilinged restaurant. Andrew ordered them each a Sazerac.

"Rumor has it that his cocktail was invented here," Andrew said as he held his glass to hers.

He insisted on ordering for her, and she acquiesced as she wasn't familiar with Creole cuisine, but she also enjoyed this new feeling of being taken care of.

After a warm greeting, the bartender proceeded to put on a show. He balanced a sugar cube on an ornate, slotted spoon and drizzled cognac and then Peychaud's bitters over it until the cube dissolved. After adding ice to two martini glasses, he stirred the cognac mixture thirty times, as was customary, he said.

He then swirled the absinthe to coat the chilled martini glasses, rubbed a lemon twist around each rim, and then dangled the twist from the side. For the finale, he strained the stirred mixture into the glasses.

Carolyn sipped her tongue-numbing drink, which tasted of fennel and pepper, while Andrew downed his in one gulp.

"Bring me the real stuff, Harry," Andrew said to the bartender.

The bartender shuffled a few bottles below the bar and brought up a sleek black bottle with two drooping green wings and the words Fe'e Magique printed on its neck. He poured a tumbler half-full of the green liquid and set it down on the bar with a loud knock.

"The flaming green fairy," he announced in a carnival huckster-like voice. He looked over at Carolyn and winked. "He always brings in the business, that one does," he said, nodding at Andrew.

Andrew dipped the cube in the green liquid and then balanced it on the spoon straddling the glass. He lit the cube on fire, and as a crowd gathered, the sugar flashed up in a burning blue flame. As the sugar melted, Andrew dropped it into the glass, setting the absinthe on fire. He set the spoon aside, brought the drink to his lips, and gulped back the flaming mixture. As the patrons in the bar oohed and clapped, Andrew looked around and smiled.

"The flaming green fairy," he announced, nodding at the applause.

Before long, the bar was bustling with patrons ordering the flaming green fairy. However, the sleek black bottle with the drooping green wings had made its way back behind the counter and a cheaper version of absinthe was being set on fire.

Most of the alcohol would burn away as most people hesitated too long before splashing the fiery liquid toward their face.

Andrew didn't seem to have that fear.

The bartender wouldn't give him a tab. "You made me money!" he said as he waved away Andrew's cash.

Andrew left a hundred-dollar bill on the bar, shook hands all around, and then escorted Carolyn out. She could still hear the racket half way down the block.

"That was fun!" she said.

The next stop was a lively jazz bar, where again, Andrew seemed to know everyone. Each member in the jazz group gave him a slick handshake or a thumbs-up sign as he walked in. Once they noticed Carolyn, they all gave nods of approval.

As soon as they sat down, a waitress hurried over, carrying a tray with two large glasses of a frothy white concoction known as a Ramos Gin Fizz. The froth continued to grow up out of the glass after the waitress set down the drinks.

Behind the waitress, a waiter delivered a tray of Oysters Rockefeller, oysters baked in their shells with buttery herb breadcrumbs. He also dropped off a basket of shrimp and okra hush puppies. Not a fan of oysters, although never having tried them, Carolyn placed one on her plate and forked a few crumbs of the buttery crust into her mouth. She couldn't eat the horrible thing, but she didn't want to appear rude.

"Um. I love these hushpuppies," she said as she dipped a crispy fried cornbread ball in the creamy remoulade sauce, heavy on horseradish and capers, while swaying to the bluesy rhythm. "This is good too," she said as she sipped the Cocktail.

The Ramos Gin Fizz was more Carolyn's type of drink. It was fruity and creamy with frothy foam formed by egg whites. She'd sipped half of it and eaten two more hushpuppies when Andrew stood up and touched her arm.

"Time to sober up with some chicory coffee."

He held her hand and led her out into the early evening street bustle while commenting on the historical significance of different buildings as they passed. A short late-summer shower had fallen while they'd been in the dark tavern. It had caused the narrow, brick-paved streets of the Vieux Carré to hiss and steam, wafting up a faint odor of urine.

"Piss and garlic," Andrew said with a laugh. "The unique aroma of the Quarter. Even after a hurricane, the stench remains."

Carolyn noticed that the odor disappeared as soon as they'd left Bourbon Street, however.

Intricate, ornate wrought iron railings of floral and leafy design adorned the second story balconies where lush ferns hung on every building. Overflowing flower boxes of begonias and bromeliads decorated the lacy iron scrollwork while sprigs of ivy dangled down toward the street in an effort to join the festivities.

Colorful artists with their finished works hanging from the gate surrounding Jackson Square were busy creating masterpieces or hawking the ones they'd finished that morning.

Street performers were setting up again after the brief shower as Andrew and Carolyn walked past Chartres Street in front of St. Louis Cathedral. They made a right turn on Saint Ann Street and headed toward the river.

"Pirate's Alley." Andrew pointed as they walked by. "Now, that's the way to live. Arghh, A pirate's life for me," he sang.

"Like Jean Lafitte, for instance. He helped General Andrew Jackson defend New Orleans against the British in 1815 using his smuggling pirate ships. There's the general now," he said as they passed a bronze statue of Andrew Jackson waving his hat from his rearing horse in the middle of the square. "Scoundrels never get the credit they deserve!"

The piercing crack of a screen door slamming on its frame caused Andrew to jerk and duck down as if he were avoiding a bullet.

"Why so jumpy?" Carolyn asked him with a concerned smile.

"Too many movies." He laughed.

Drips still fell from the green and white scalloped awning of the Café Du Monde covering the outdoor seating area.

"Wait under the overhang around the corner," Andrew said. "I'll be right back. Café au lait ok?" he asked.

Carolyn watched him make his way through the crowd to place their order. The Café was overflowing with patrons using the shelter as an escape from the rain as they lingered over their coffee and beignets.

He returned with two cafés au lait and a plate of dusted beignets.

"Let's go sit by the river. It's a mess in there," he said.

Powder from the hot, fried dough puffs blew onto his shirt with every word.

"Don't inhale while eating these." He laughed, but he looked down at his shirt with a grimace.

Carolyn took the plate and followed him to a bench next to the Civil War cannon on the platform. He handed her a few napkins with the coffee cups.

"Put these down. I'm sure the bench is still wet."

She was glad he'd brought a handful.

They sat and sipped their coffee while listening to a three-piece street group strum cheerful reggae tunes at the foot of the steps.

A pretty but weather worn white carriage pulled up and stopped in front of Jackson Square across from them.

"Mmm, what a wonderful day," Carolyn said.

Andrew turned to her and smiled. "Yes. Yes it is," he said as he gazed into her eyes.

They talked a long time that evening.

Andrew spoke with concern as he asked her everything about her life. He listened as she told him about her family and her business. He leaned in close and held her hand as she talked about her brother's passing. When her voice quivered, he wrapped his arm around her side and pulled her snug to his chest. She felt safe and comfortable when she rested her face on his shoulder.

Her heart surrendered with the slow warmth of a winter sunrise when he reached over to kiss away a tear.

He understood. He asked so many questions. He cared.

Like a colossal hazy orb of a fortune teller's ball, the smoky yellow moon transcended the highest of spire of the cathedral across the square. The light cast a shimmery veil, enveloping them in a private magical spell. Carolyn was feeling fortunate that her fate had led her to such a wonderful soul. She felt comforted for the first time since her brother's death.

Andrew grasped her hands and began to talk of the wonderful future they might have together. His beautiful words strung together as if they were a treasured necklace of inherited pearls. Timeless, priceless, irreplaceable.

The thought this was all happening so fast didn't seem to matter. It was a relief not to feel grief. Carolyn melted into the brief respite of pain.

Her experience in romance was limited to a brief marriage after high school. She'd been blissful and in love until the afternoon she came home from work and found her husband in their bed with a rather unattractive girl they'd both known in high school. The girl had always had a crush on her husband. He dumped her after the divorce, but by that time, it was far too late to salvage any feelings.

And thank goodness she thought, as she looked into Andrew's eyes.

CAROL GOODNIGHT

Andrew's fervent campaign to win her with extravagant dinners and wine continued for the next week. Well-known chefs from every new hot spot in the Big Easy invited him to taste their latest creations - on the house, of course.

Apparently people with real money never had to pay.

Andrew seemed to know everyone. And everyone seemed impressed with him.

Carolyn realized, even though she knew it was shallow, she enjoyed this VIP treatment. And Andrew cared for her, maybe even loved her. He had rescued her at her lowest moment.

She shook her head and sighed. *I can't believe how lucky I am.*

CHAPTER 8

A rare and expensive copy of John Milton's *Paradise Lost* arrived with a massive bouquet of pink peonies the evening before Carolyn and Andrew's fourth dinner date. Andrew knocked at the door as Carolyn was opening the book. She reached to kiss his face as she thanked him.

Andrew took the book from her hand and held it to his lips. With a somber tone, he said, "One day I shall read this to our children."

A flush covered Carolyn's cheeks at the thought of having children with Andrew. She looked away to hide her face.

"I'll keep it safe until then," she stammered as she pulled open her suitcase and slid the antique book into a secret compartment.

Having never read the classic, Carolyn didn't realize until much later that it wasn't at all suitable for young children.

Over dinner that evening he explained that the donation of a long abandoned sugar plantation in St. Mary's parish, owned by Andrew's family, was the reason Andrew found himself in Louisiana. He'd invited Carolyn along to do a cursory inspection before donating the property to a Louisiana land trust.

"It'll be a nice little tax deduction," he'd said. "The plantation is edged into the southern Louisiana bayou where the residents considered themselves Cajuns and primarily spoke French.

"French Canadians were the main founders of the bayou culture, with contributions from Spanish, German, African, Irish, and Native Americans. They braided together much like the Mississippi River-fed streams of the bayou to form the modern Cajun culture," Andrew explained.

"It'll be a long drive and then we'll travel by boat through the swamp. The remote location is the major reason for the donation instead of a sale. My grandmother was fond of wasting my family's money," he said.

Carolyn didn't noticed the snide remark. She'd been swept away with all of Andrew's attention and saw life as an adventure opening before her again. She was excited and looking forward to spending another day with him.

Andrew's family had never actually lived at the plantation, he explained.

"Grandmother Rebecca instigated the silly purchase after seeing *Gone with the Wind*, a popular movie at the time. This was to be their summer get-a-way, and she'd planned to entertain her guests in a grand southern style. She'd even ordered two carriages so guests could take long carriage rides through the 250-year-old oak-lined lane that led up to the mansion."

"As the story goes, she was so caught up in the romance of it all that she'd even insisted grandfather grow a mustache matching Clark Gable's. Apparently it never grew quite as glamorous as Clark's did, and I've heard he actually resembled Hitler more than Rhett Butler," he laughed.

"There's a picture somewhere," he laughed again. "I'll have to find it."

"Anyway, Grandmother spent exactly one week in the rambling old mansion, overseeing painting and repairs, before the oppressive heat and the fire ants got to her. Her last night at the plantation was spent crying, scratching, and sweating."

He busted out laughing and continued, still laughing.

"I heard that on the plane back to Los Angeles the next morning she sniped, 'The moment we get home, you are to shave off that asinine mustache!'"

At this point, Andrew bent over with laughter. After he calmed down, he added, "She never returned to her Tara. In fact, she never permitted the subject to be spoken of again in her presence."

Carolyn chuckled at Andrew's imitation of his grandmother. The story struck her funny. Rich people and their troubles. She had to agree with Andrew's grandmother, though. Renovating an old place certainly had a romantic appeal.

Even in the best of situations, it's hard work. Especially without road access. When you add the sweltering humidity of August in the South, not to mention the teeth with wings, otherwise known as no-seeums, it was easy to see how the dream died so soon.

CAROL GOODNIGHT

CHAPTER 9

Andrew was waiting for her in front of the hotel next to his shiny, spotless Bentley. As he held her door, he leaned in to kiss her cheek. Carolyn couldn't stop smiling.

Once through the narrow streets of the quarter, they headed west on Route 90 toward Boscoyo. The two lanes of highway cut through the low-lying plain with high brush and pine forests on either side. In several places, the highway lifted them up and carried them over and through the marshy cypress swamps. The scenery was charming with only a farm clearing or a tiny group of homes to break up the never-ending forest view.

As they entered the center of Boscoyo, an isolated little burg where seven or eight waterways converged, two large bridges appeared. An old bridge, and an older one still, crossed the river side by side.

Fear gripped Carolyn. "Ah." Carolyn groaned. "I hate scary old bridges."

As they reached the highest point on the first bridge, Andrew slowed the car to a stop.

"Look how far over the bayou you can see," he said.

"Andrew, please. Just hurry across. Please?" Carolyn pleaded.

Andrew came to a complete stop and stared at the side of the bridge.

"I once saw a man fall to his death from a bridge," he said. The faraway look in his eye and his voice, edged in disgust, did little to calm Carolyn's nerves.

"Please, Andrew. Keep driving. Please?" she asked again.

Andrew sat staring at the bridge.

"Andrew, this is not funny! It's not very considerate to scare me like this! I've always hated old bridges!"

Andrew cocked his head at an awkward angle and swerved his neck in the manner of a curious reptile to look at her. She could almost see something sinister in his eyes. But as he met her concerned gaze, his cold, ice-blue stare softened into something more familiar.

"I'm sorry, dear. I thought you would enjoy the view from here," he said in a smooth monotone.

Looking over the side of the bridge again, his upper lip curled into the slightest snarl before he turned his face back to the road and gunned the engine.

He screeched to a stop at a small diner on the other side of the bridge. Carolyn's expression remained pinched.

The flat roofed, one story building had large white awnings that covered three picture windows. One window was missing, however, and a piece of plywood hung in its place. Most of the restaurant, freshly painted white, still sported a worn and dirty blue trim.

A happy-faced red shrimp with bulging eyes and a tall chef's hat on a large hand-painted sign greeted them as they entered the five-space parking lot. Well, it would have been five spaces if the dumpster hadn't taken up one of the spots.

"These little rat holes have the best food," Andrew said.

Carolyn was still annoyed with him for stopping on the bridge. But he hopped out of the car, and with a bit of a limp, walked around to open her door. He held her hand and welcomed her to the diner. In an exaggerated French Creole accent he said, "Byenveni, beautiful madam."

"What does that mean?" Carolyn asked. "And why are you limping?"

"It means welcome. I'm sorry I scared you. Please forgive me. I'll die of a broken heart if you don't, beautiful madam," he said. "And I'm limping because even one of the most expensive automobiles in the world isn't soft enough for my precious behind."

Carolyn grinned and pushed her irritation out of her mind.

Everyone has demons. She certainly had plenty of her own. Hating bridges was only one of them.

The waitress greeted them with a thick, cheerful Cajun accent. Without looking up, Andrew ordered.

"Two colas. Two cubes of ice. Each. No more. No less. We don't need snow cones."

A quizzical look crossed Carolyn's face. Andrew peeked over the menu and chuckled who a boy that had made a not-so-funny joke.

"They cheat you by giving you frozen water and I HATE being cheated," he laughed.

Again, Carolyn wondered at how unusual people with money acted.

Andrew smiled at her and winked. They both ordered the Cajun shrimp and grits. It was the first time she'd ever tried the succulent, spicy shrimp dish served over creamy cheese grits. It made her top ten list of favorites after only a few bites.

After lunch, they drove to the nearby marina. Andrew had arranged for a boat rental before they'd arrived.

A twelve-foot, flat-bottomed duck boat with an old twenty-five horsepower Johnson outboard was waiting for them at the water's edge. Silver aluminum glinted through the dark army-green paint where it had sustained dings and dents by years of use on the bayou. A quick payment and they were off. Andrew held her hand and steadied the boat as she stepped in. She was thankful she'd worn jeans and brought a wallet instead of the sundress and clutch she'd been thinking about. Especially after she'd slipped while stepping into the boat.

"Such a gentleman," she said.

Meanwhile, she wondered why he had chosen this boat, when with all his money, he could've rented any boat there.

"My pleasure, beautiful lady." He kissed her hand.

After a couple of quick jerks on the pull cord, the engine fired up to idle. Andrew looked at her with a self-satisfied grin. "But of course, on the first try," he said.

Carolyn only laughed. It would be rude to point out it had actually taken a couple of tries.

Andrew stood with his feet planted, holding the stabilizing bar with his left hand, his right hand on the throttle. He grabbed the tiller and eased a turn on the throttle. After it fired up, he steered the front of the boat down river toward one of the larger waterway canal-like entrances. Carolyn situated herself sidesaddle on the small seat at the front of the boat. She glanced at the passing industrial-looking shoreline, thinking the boat was noisy but pleasant enough. She still wondered at its choice as they eased down the river.

Without warning, the boat roared into full throttle. As the front of the boat lifted out of the water, Carolyn grasped its sides with all her strength. With the boat's front end pointing toward the sky, three or four feet from the surface, she turned to steady herself and face Andrew. She braced her feet on the bench seat in front of her to keep from sliding.

As the front of the boat planed out and dropped closer to the water Carolyn relaxed her grip. Andrew looked at her with a mischievous smile. He mouthed the word "sorry" while paying no attention at all to the "no wake zone" signs.

Carolyn tried to tell him to slow down, but he couldn't hear her over the irritating, high decibel noise, and she couldn't seem to catch his eye without letting go of the sides of the boat. He zoomed past homes and small shacks built on stilts over the water's edge without so much as a glance toward her. So she resigned herself to sit back and watch the small town fade behind them.

Carolyn noticed they were fast approaching an old, rather large fisherman in a small wooden pirogue about twenty feet off shore. His hat rested down over his face, shielding it from the sun. He seemed to be doing more napping than fishing. As he heard the loud engine roaring his way, he stood to watch as their boat sped toward him. With all of his weight, his boat only cleared about five inches above the waterline. He waved his hand back and forth in an effort to get them to slow down. As they came closer, he shook his fists.

A big wave from Andrew's wake rolled toward the shoreline. The fisherman sat down, grabbed both sides of his small boat and prepared for the impact coming his way.

Carolyn wasn't sure if Andrew hadn't seen the boater or if he didn't realize the wave would be so large. As the swell from their boat reached him, the fisherman's small boat rocked to one side, causing water to splash in on the other side. The little boat bobbed up and down a few times before steadying itself.

Carolyn looked back at Andrew. There was no expression on his face.

Couldn't he see what was going on? Did he need glasses?

He reached to smooth his perfect, golden-highlighted hair as it whipped about in the wind. He looked straight past her, without making eye contact.

Carolyn saw the fisherman raise his hand to make an obscene gesture. Her eyes widened, and she jerked her face away.

The canal narrowed as they buzzed forward. After almost passing a fork, Andrew made a quick left without slowing the boat. The turn caused the boat to spray water out to their right while dipping over the edge to their left.

Carolyn had had enough.

"Andrew! Knock it off!"

He chuckled and again mouthed the word, "sorry."

The canal grew shallow as it narrowed and the current slowed. The forest grew thick over them, blocking out the sun.

As the water grew shallow, the propeller revved and whined. They'd hit mud. Andrew turned off the engine and propped up the outboard motor. Carolyn closed her eyes in relief at the silence. Her ears were still ringing when she felt a sharp nudge in her back. When she turned around, Andrew was handing her a paddle.

Andrew's strength was obvious as he rowed behind her, gliding them through the water. His taut biceps gleamed from sweat below the sleeves of his white designer polo shirt. Carolyn looked at him. He was so strong and smart. And handsome.

Billions of tiny duckweed leaves covered the surface of the slow moving water as their boat glided over the thick emerald carpet. A drake, with his mate trailing behind, paddled in and around the large cypress knobs sticking out from the edge of the swamp. Their trail, cut through the thick pea-soup surface, immediately closed in behind them. The lively, pleasant song of the water thrush and the paddles dipping in and out of the shallow creek broke the stillness under the lush canopy.

A pair of alligator eyes, the only sign of the large reptilian beast that lay resting below the surface, blinked, then stared at the passing boat. Carolyn stared back at him.

As they rounded the next bend, the canal widened, and the thick forest above the water opened to form a haunting cathedral of tall cypress trees laced in thick Spanish moss.

The graceful, swaying moss reminded Carolyn of a tattered bride's gown from long ago, draped and waiting for an errant groom who never showed. Wild ruby-throated orchid sprays in tones of pink festooned the shady grotto like tossed aside bridesmaid bouquets.

The delicate wings of the white ibis flying in and out of the rookery to their left were like fresh hankies to wipe tears in this imagined melancholy sanctuary.

Carolyn stopped rowing and gazed in awe.

"I've never seen anything so lovely," she said. "Andrew, this is beautiful. Thank you for inviting me to this place."

"I knew you would love it, my dear. It is beautiful. Almost as lovely as you are," he said.

Carolyn smiled.

But a tiny, yet niggling thought in the back of her mind crept onto her face and her smile faded a bit.

They were out here in the bayou away from civilization, all alone.

How well do I really know Andrew? she wondered while keeping her eye on a large snake that writhed out of the water and slithered over a fan of orchids before twining its wet body around a thick tree branch that hung low above the water.

As Andrew paddled on, she took up the paddle to steer again. The canal grew wider and deeper. As the canopy disappeared behind them, they found themselves in the blistering sun again. Andrew plopped the engine back into the water and pulled the cord. Only twice this time. Once again they were cutting through the water at full tilt. Carolyn rolled her eyes at the loud, obnoxious noise of the boat engine. It was all the more horrible for ruining the beautiful nature sounds of the swamp.

She pulled her paddle up with a sigh and set it behind her. Ten long, loud minutes later, a row of small buildings came into view ahead on the right. Identical tiny red brick houses lined the water in a narrow row. All but two had matching metal corrugated roofs in various stages of rust. Those two stood roofless. She realized they had been slave quarters.

A family of nutria, or marsh dogs, was digging a hole right above the water line. One large fellow, probably the patriarch, carried a large stalk of long-abandoned sugar cane under his elongated yellow front teeth. He glanced at them with disinterest as he climbed down the bank with his lunch.

Carolyn hoped this was the plantation, but Andrew didn't slow down. She looked back at him to ask if they were almost there.

He stared straight ahead. He didn't meet her eye.

Before she turned back around to face the front, she saw him grab the metal stabilizing bar and brace himself. In the next moment, they hit a large cypress knee that extended out of the water about two and a half feet.

With a sudden jolt and a quick dead stop, Carolyn flew off the front end of the boat. For a few seconds, she felt suspended in the air, limb's flailing, gasping in horror, before the dark, warm swamp water engulfed her. In those few moments, the sound of the boat engine died away and the only thing she heard was her own pulse throbbing in her ears.

She thrashed to the surface, screaming and choking as panic hammered her heart against her ribs. Salty blood mixed with acrid swamp water and duckweed as she crunched her teeth over her lips to clamp shut her gaping mouth.

Big black splotches covered her eyes as she stretched her chin out of the water and gasped. She flailed her arms, choking on the acrid mud water and duckweed. Her legs twitched back and forth as she tried to gain footing in the bottom slime.

A dangling leech clinging to her left eyelid obscured what appeared to be a ghastly grin on Andrew's calm and relaxed face.

Impossible! she thought in confusion as she scratched and clawed her face to remove the disgusting creature.

Impossible!

She began a furious dog-paddle toward the bank. But the slick sound of something scurrying along the muddy embankment paralyzed her. She wedged her foot through the bottom slime and stood frozen in panic. Mosquitoes hummed and gnats hoarded around her face in the humid stench of decaying vegetation stirred up from the bottom muck by her footsteps. A nasty, giant horse fly hunting for a blood meal ripped a chunk of flesh from her forehead.

Carolyn's arms flailed and an unfamiliar shriek screeched through her muddy lips.

"Oh my God!" she screamed. "Help me!"

She jerked her leg to move, but it caught knee deep in muck and held as tight as a Chinese finger trap.

"Aghh!" she huffed as she leaned forward and dragged one foot to the top of the mud and then the other. Using her shins, she balanced her weight to get leverage and continued to slog forward on her knees to keep from sinking.

Every move created a sucking pressure vacuum that made the effort to move forward exhausting.

"Help!" she cried as she clawed at the thin weeds in the black slime of the bank. The stems and roots pulled free in her hands. Several mysterious plops registered in her mind as big fat frogs jumping to safety. At least that's what she hoped they were.

"Andrew! Help me!" she cried.

"Climb up to the shore, Carolyn!"

"I can't. I can't get a grip. It's slime!"

The boat continued floating down the canal. Andrew stared, not making any move to help.

She turned and swam toward him. As she got closer, the calm look on Andrew's face became distressed. He stood up and glanced around both shores. As she reached for the side of the boat, she saw him reach down for the paddle.

The boat rocked hard toward her. Andrew tried to balance himself, still grasping the paddle, while teetering back and forth.

Thump!

Andrew's head hit the side of the boat with a thick thud before he splashed into the murky water. The boat rolled and tipped upside down. Carolyn thrust her arms and legs through the water, searching to find him.

As the upturned boat settled, Andrew floated to the surface next to her. Carolyn breathed a sigh of relief.

She grabbed his shirt and pulled him to the upturned boat. With his face floating above the water, Carolyn noticed his forehead was bleeding, and he didn't appear to be conscious.

Even though she kicked as hard as she could, the boat continued drifting at a leisurely pace.

As the clearing for the slave homestead ended, the remnants of a dock came into view. Carolyn kicked harder. Grabbing what remained of the last rung on the dock, she let go of the boat. It floated away.

"Andrew? Andrew? Are you OK? Andrew, please?" she yelled.

She watched the blood trickle from a small gash on his forehead as she clung to the rotten wood. It didn't look too deep, but an egg-size lump was turning blue beneath it.

He groaned.

"Andrew, are you OK? Andrew, I'm so sorry. I tipped the boat. Andrew?" she cried.

She tried to hoist him up out of the water, but he was twice her weight.

He groaned again.

A rustling sound from above startled Carolyn.

"Lemme hep y'all, missy," said a gravelly voiced old woman.

At least that's what Carolyn thought she said. Her accent was as thick as the duckweed. The old woman got down on her knees, and with two thin, spidery arms, she grabbed Andrew by his armpits. As she hoisted him up, Carolyn pushed him from below. The old woman seemed to have superhuman strength, and a moment later Andrew's stomach slapped the muddy bank with a loud flop.

Carolyn climbed up what remained of the old dock to see him trying to sit up.

"Lie back, Andrew," Carolyn said as she crawled over to him. She held his head in her hands and used her thigh as a pillow. Andrew closed his eyes and groaned again.

CAROL GOODNIGHT

"I brung the wagon for ya," said the old woman. "But looks like we'll be needin' it for him."

"Thank God you were here," Carolyn said, looking at the old woman for the first time.

The woman stood with a sense of authority and an elegance exuding from her posture. With her patrician nose and the contour of her high cheekbones still evident, the skin around her jowls sagged a bit.

A deep scar from her right ear, across her cheek and through her left eye, ended somewhere in the purple scarf wrapped around her forehead. Carolyn's eyes widened as she did a double-take.

"A sickle done it," the woman said, familiar with that look of surprise.

"The last beatin' ole Antione Galafate, my dearly departed husband, give anybody," she said with a cackle.

Nodding toward the swamp she said, "Gators et him."

She cackled again.

Carolyn's eyes widened as she realized she'd just crawled from that same swamp.

"They call me Lady Ce'cil round these parts," she said, pronouncing it SeeSeel, growling out the last syllable.

"Let's get his highness in the wagon." She gripped Andrew's arm and the back of his shirt. He was waking up.

Carolyn turned her attention back to Andrew as she helped Lady Ce'cil get him into the cart. The gash on his head was bleeding steadily. She looked for something to wipe it with, but everything she was wearing was saturated with mud. She decided it best to let it bleed until she could get some clean water. They laid him down in the wagon and propped his head on his arm.

Carolyn wondered how far they had to go as she pushed and Lady Ce'cil pulled the old wagon. The bees continued to buzz while the dragonflies flitted atop the tall grass, not affected in the least by the small drama playing out beside them as they passed.

Andrew groaned again.

Carolyn thought about what the old woman said to her.

"What did you mean, you brought the wagon for me, but we could use it for Andrew? Did Andrew tell you I was coming?"

"I don't know no Andrew, missy. I only knowd you was comin'."

"Me? You knew I was coming? I wasn't even sure until yesterday I was coming myself. How did you know if Andrew didn't tell you?"

"I see things, missy. I see things," she said. "Sometimes I'm wrong. And sometimes things change. Thank the good lord on that, but I got somethin' important to tell you. We'll have us a nice chat after we get this fella looked after."

The grassy path led them by a small overgrown stick-fenced graveyard.

"Them's the slaves," Lady Ce'cil announced. "The white folk is buried in a nice section next to the boilin' house, so's they can smell the sweet cain cookin. Well, used to."

Nodding her head toward several high places in the earth scattered along the path, she tugged the wagon with both of her strong maple-colored arms extended out behind her.

"Civil war soldiers buried in them graves," she said.

The path eventually led to the back of the enormous main house.

"Is this Andrew's plantation?" Carolyn asked.

Lady Ce'cil didn't answer.

They passed by the kitchen garden filled with overgrown herbs, a few tomato plants and several rows of lettuce. Rose bushes that appeared to have been growing wild for quite some time, resulted in a rolling thicket of yellow that surrounded the entire large flagstone patio. The plantation home stood three stories high with the third story dormers looking out into the treetops of ancient goliath oaks.

"Whoa! This is beyond beautiful," Carolyn said to herself, as she held the door open while Lady Ce'cil wheeled Andrew into the kitchen.

The food prep area of the kitchen was to the left of the large oblong room. Lady Ce'cil rolled the wagon up to the sink, grabbed a kitchen towel and wiped Andrew's head. She nodded toward the refrigerator. Carolyn pulled out an ice tray and wrapped the cubes in a clean dish towel. She placed the make-shift ice bag over the small gash in Andrew's head and he opened his eyes.

"What happened?" he asked.

"Oh, Andrew, I'm so sorry. You hit your head on the boat after I fell out."

He mumbled words Carolyn couldn't understand, and then he reached for the sides of the wagon to pull himself up. Lady Cecil poured him a large glass of sweet tea and gave him a tablet to swallow.

"Make your head right," she said.

Andrew took a drink of tea and examined the tablet. The small writing on the pill was apparently familiar to him as he popped it in his mouth followed by a gulp of the tea. As he attempted to pull himself up out of the wagon, he looked at Lady Cecil.

"Who the hell are you?" he asked.

"Ahhh. I am Lady Ce'cil. I look after this place. Have for forty years," she said.

"More like a squatter, I'd say," he replied with a grimace.

"Andrew! She saved our lives!" Carolyn said.

"I'm sorry, dear. I'm not myself," he said as he pulled himself out of the wagon and wiped strings of algae from his hair. He steadied himself. "Where the hell is the shower? I need to get this scum off of me."

The old woman walked to the kitchen door and then looked back, nodding her head toward the next room in a "follow me" motion. Lady Ce'cil led them through the tall doorway into the dining room then on into the enormous three-story foyer.

A bridal staircase with hand-carved railing curved around

each side of the grand entryway. The aged dark wood created a dramatic landing at the top of the second floor and an equally dramatic but smaller landing at the top of the third floor. Carolyn stopped to look around the cavernous room. She marveled at the craftsmanship while she balanced from one foot to the next, trying to limit the puddle collecting from her dripping clothes.

The walls were a faded light sage, stamped with a delicate filigree pattern in a darker green to give a look of wallpaper. Dust fairies caught in the light streaming through a large round window over the double entrance doors twinkled as they danced above her.

"What a grand place," Carolyn said.

"Ain't so grand when you gots to clean all them spider webs," Lady Cecil answered.

She was already at the top of the first staircase, waiting for them, as Andrew held the railing and climbed the steps one step at a time. It was apparent he had a problem with his hip. He had been masking it well until now.

Lady Cecil led Andrew to the first room at the top of the stairs.

"You wait here," she told Carolyn as she led Andrew into the room and closed the door.

A few moments later, she emerged and bustled past Carolyn. She headed to the other side of the landing toward the farthest room from the staircase. She flung open the door to a cheery yellow room and stepped aside as Carolyn walked in.

A handmade carpet with swirls of faded yellow roses matching the faded wall paint lay in front of the fireplace. A gentle breeze through the open window blew delicate ripples in the sheer fabric hanging around a large canopy bed. Fresh yellow roses filled the large hand-painted washbasin sitting on an ornate white table in front of the window.

"This room's for you," said Lady Ce'cil. "There's some dry duds for ya in the bathroom."

CAROL GOODNIGHT

With that, she walked out the door and closed it behind her. Carolyn looked around the room, thinking how odd it was that out here, beyond nowhere, a guest room had been readied for her.
A throwback in time, the room was charming until she stepped into the bathroom. The 50's style update of gaudy yellow tiles and the aluminum and glass shower doors was a welcome sight, however, as the drying mud was beginning to itch.

Carolyn stepped into the shower in her wet clothes and undressed. She reached down and touched the chain her brother had given her, still clasped on her ankle. Relieved, she sighed.

She rinsed her clothes and wrung them out before immersing herself in the steamy, clean water. The pipes rattled and shook, sputtering the water as she put shampoo in her hair.

"Oh, great," she grumbled.

She stood waiting in the trickle, trying to process what had happened on the boat. Something wasn't right. She felt it. She knew it.

She was actually afraid for a moment out there alone with Andrew. Even before the boat hit the cypress knee. And why did he hit that? It stuck out of the water a good two and a half feet.

The shower surged on, and she rinsed her hair, hurrying to finish before it died off again. After drying herself, she slipped on the long cotton dress hanging from the towel rack. She stood in the window, her brain on autopilot, and ran her fingers through her hair in the breeze.

How did that woman know she was coming if she didn't know Andrew? How did she know they'd need a wagon and that she'd need a clean dress?

As she headed back down to the kitchen, admiring the architecture of the massive old place, her questions multiplied.

Lady Ce'cil was in the kitchen, arranging a large silver tray with a pitcher of tea, sandwiches, and cookies.

"Let's go set a spell on the front porch," she said.

Carolyn opened one of the heavy front doors and pushed it

aside for Lady Ce'cil and her tray. After serving the tea and sandwiches, Lady Ce'cil sat down.

"Listen here. I know you already done had you a good ole hard time in life. More'n your share. Me too, but I'm old now. You still got some life to live. I'm a givin' you a warnin'. Your brother, he's a lookin' after you. He's says you're in danger. You need to look inside."

"What do you mean, my brother's looking after me? He's—" Carolyn could hardly say the word. She swallowed so she could speak without crying.

"He's dead. He was killed in a car accident."

Lady Ce'cil sighed. "I know he's dead. I know. I told ya, I see things. Dead things, live things."

"You've seen my brother?" she asked, leaning forward.

"Is he OK? Did he suffer? Why did he have to go so soon? I never had the chance to say goodbye. Does he know I loved him?" Carolyn asked, her lip trembling.

"Missy, you're forgettin' the important thing," Lady Ce'cil said with a frown.

"You're in danger! You know it in your heart!"

"Follow your heart. Look inside," Carolyn wondered aloud. She leaned back, thinking about the inscription on the anklet that her brother had sent her.

"My brother had that inscribed on this, to remind me of the courage he thought I had," she said as she stretched out her ankle.

"Could it mean anything else?"

"Damn if I know! But when I get a sign, I learnt the hard way to pay it mind," she said, drawing her pointer and index finger across her face alongside the sickle slash.

"But…" Carolyn started.

"I only know what I told ya. Ain't no sense askin' me more."

"He thinks I'm in danger? What kind of danger?" Carolyn said, as her voice trailed off. "Not Andrew?" she asked. "I barely know him. He'd have no reason to put me in danger. I mean, he's a terrible driver for sure, but…"

The woman shook her head and looked at the ground. Her voice grew soft.

"Sorry, chile. There ain't no more."

After a quiet pause, Lady Ce'cil faced her. A kindness shown through her eyes.

"Sit out here till dark if you want. Nothin's gonna bother you. Still enough blue on the ceilin' to keep the Haints away."

Carolyn's voice trembled. "Haints?" was the only word she got out.

"Yes, missy, Haints. They be restless spirits of the dead who ain't moved on from this world into the next. Why, I sees Ole Antione's face, my dearly departed husband, you know, reflected in the window right there many a night. I sees his mug all twisted up in agony, same face he had when that gator took the first bite outa his mean ole hide." Lady Ce'cil's dark skeletal finger bobbed up and down as she pointed at the reflection in the window.

"Comes back every full moon. Haints cain't cross water so we trick'em with blue paint. You be safe out here, all right. I'm a check on his highness and hit the hay. He be out till mornin'. You mind what I say, now," she said, still wagging her gnarled finger as she walked back into the house.

Carolyn sat rocking the porch chair and looked out toward the front entrance. The mammoth oaks on either side of the dusty lane bent their branches over to one another, forming a natural tunnel. As dusk stole light from the sky, the branches darkened and blurred. A whippoorwill calling out a mournful cry from the marsh added a melody to the chirping crickets and nasal complaints of the swamp frogs. The low bellowing B-flat grunt of a nearby alligator finished out the rhythm section of the eerie nocturnal symphony.

Carolyn watched as the mist rose from the damp ground and swirled into the trees. The graceful sweeping branches seemed to turn into cadaverous clawing arms with their bony fingers scratching toward one another. She looked up at the peeling bluish-green ceiling and hoped what Lady Ce'cil had said about the Haints was true. Even though she'd never heard of them before, she didn't want them around.

The war between the mosquitoes and the citronella candle on the tray was beginning in earnest. So, after one too many bites, Carolyn called it a night. She locked the huge double doors behind her, left the tray in the kitchen, and then headed up to her room. She brought the candle with her as she didn't want to disturb anyone to find the light switches.

The door to Andrew's room creaked as she opened it to check on him. He was mumbling in a disturbed tone.

"Andrew, are you OK?" she whispered.

Andrew kept mumbling.

He must be talking in his sleep; she turned to walk away.

"Die, you bastard!" he cried out.

Carolyn stopped for a moment and then rushed to her room. She locked the door behind her and pulled on it, making sure it was secure. She set the candle on the fireplace, closed the window and climbed up into the high bed. A mosquito buzzed by her ear, so she climbed back down and pulled the sheer curtains closed around the bed. After getting comfortable, with the soft sheets pulled up around her nose to ward off further bites, the itching started.

Rebecca, Andrew's grandmother, had made the right decision, Carolyn thought. This place, with its swamps and bugs and eerie-sounding birds and spooky trees, was beautiful by day. But by night, out here, nowhere, it was damn scary.

Carolyn lay awake most of the night, listening to the noises and the groans inside the house. It all seemed too familiar as she hoped there wasn't a southern version of Raw Head and Bloody Bones hiding in the attic. After concentrating on the noises drifting back and forth between the gnarled and wizened oak trees outside, she finally passed out for about an hour around four a.m.

CAROL GOODNIGHT

Rebecca, Andrew's grandmother, had made the right decision. This place, with its swamps and bugs and eerie-sounding birds and spooky trees, was beautiful by day. But by night, out here, nowhere, it was damn scary.

CHAPTER 10

The aroma of coffee wafted into her room later that morning to wake her from a light slumber. When she stepped into to the kitchen she noticed the door to the patio open. She looked out to see Andrew sitting with a scowl and staring into the space as his fingers clenched a cup of coffee.

"Good morning, Andrew. How are you feeling?"

As soon as he saw her, the scowl disappeared, and he answered cheerfully, "I'm wonderful. Glad to be alive."

"Oh my Gosh, that was terrible. Thank goodness Lady Ce'cil was here to help us," she said.

"There's no one here, Carolyn," Andrew replied, looking at her as if she were crazy.

"This place has been empty for years."

"No, Andrew, an old woman helped me pull you out of the canal. Don't you remember?"

"No, Carolyn," he answered rather firmly.

She looked at him with confusion as she watched his face grow stern. She stepped back into the kitchen to get herself a cup of coffee.

"It doesn't make any sense," she murmured to herself.

As she prepared her cup of coffee, she decided that Andrew

must have suffered a concussion and lost the memory of Lady Ce'cil. That must be the answer.

As she walked back to the patio with her coffee to explain what might have happened, a short, round man walked around the back of the house.

He tipped his hat and shouted over the thicket of rose bushes, "I'm here! I got the car out front."

"Car?" Carolyn asked, surprising the man.

"I thought this place was only accessible by boat?"

"Oh, sorry dear, I only told you that so I could show you the beauty of the bayou. It backfired on me, though, didn't it?"

Carolyn thought she saw his lip curl.

When he saw the look of concern on her face, he added, "I tried to get you alone to myself, dear." He attempted to smile. "Ouch. My head hurts," he said and looked at her with a shy grin. He stood up from the table and stretched his stiff leg. "Let's go. We've relived enough of Grandmother's nightmare. This place is gone."

Andrew walked straight through the dining room and stood waiting impatiently in the grand entrance as Carolyn hustled up the stairs to gather her clothes. He held her arm as they walked out the front door to the waiting car. He never looked back.

Andrew held the door as Carolyn stepped into the sweltering backseat. After he closed it, he walked around to the other side.

Carolyn heard the driver through the closed windows. "I thought you was comin' back alone, boss."

She couldn't hear what Andrew mumbled in response, but his arm gesture indicated he wasn't happy with the question.

Without a word, he got in the back with her, rested his head on the seat, and closed his eyes.

Carolyn didn't want to disturb him, but she had so many questions. When Andrew turned his face away from her, she realized her questions would have to wait.

As they drove around the circular drive toward the oak-lined lane, Carolyn took a last look at the century-old mansion. It echoed the romance of another era, a time where tradition and manners were all important. The high round pillars of the Greek revival plantation stood firm, gripping tight the past with a look of total abandonment. The windows gaped forlorn, anticipating the solitude that would allow them to languor once again in the mist of swirling pirate ghosts, patriot graves, and kudzu-strangled sugar cane. Longing to once more listen, in solemn secret, to the serenade of mournful creaking leviathan oaks, piercing shrill cicadas, and the anguished echo of bittersweet spirituals.

Carolyn wondered what would become of it.

A glint in one of the third-floor dormers caught her eye. She turned in the seat and leaned forward to see if she'd imagined it. The dark window panes stared back at her with the same empty-eyed gaze the stone angels bore at the cemetery.

Then she saw it again, the familiar purple color of Lady Ce'cil's scarf.

As she looked closer, the old woman wagged her finger.

"You mind what I say, now," Carolyn remembered her saying with vocal cords that sounded like bones rasping on a gravestone.

A bitter chill of fear entwined itself with an unexpected onslaught of new sadness and prickled down her spine.

When they pulled up in front of Carolyn's hotel, Andrew stepped out of the car and told the driver to wait.

"You don't need to walk me to my room, Andrew. I know you're not feeling well, and I'm exhausted myself," Carolyn said.

"I insist, my dear," Andrew replied. "I've put you through enough. You have taken good care of me. Saved my life, in fact. The least I can do is escort you to your room."

Glad she'd kept her driver's license, credit cards, and hotel room key in her jeans pocket instead of a purse that would be in floating with the gators, she unlocked her door.

The room was in shambles. Both mattresses lay slashed open

against the wall. The lamps were broken with the bases torn off. Every drawer was pulled out and lay upside down with all her clothes strewn about.

"Andrew! Look!" Carolyn shouted.

Andrew said nothing but walked around the room inspecting the damage. He leaned over the bed to the picture still hanging on the wall, pulled it out, and looked behind it.

"Why would someone do this?" Carolyn asked, near tears. She ruffled through her jumble of clothing on the floor and then checked the secret compartment of her suitcase.

She looked up at Andrew.

"The book! The beautiful book you gave me! It's gone."

She burst into tears.

Andrew wrapped his arms around her.

"It'll be all right. It'll all be all right. Don't worry about a thing," he said.

He escorted her down to the courtyard and ordered her a cup of tea before going to speak to the hotel manager. He was back a short time later with a look of satisfaction on his face.

"Carolyn. You're coming with me. We're flying back to L.A., out of this god forsaken jungle."

"What about my car?" Carolyn asked, not sure if she was ready to make such a big move with him. But Andrew had taken care of it. He told her he'd prepaid the garage fee for three months.

"After that, we can ship it home. By then you'll be so in love with me that home will be L.A. rather than some Midwest suburb," he reassured her.

Carolyn looked at Andrew as he took her hand and walked her across the tarmac to his private plane.

She barely knew him and it wasn't her style to make rash decisions. She was a contractor. She always made careful plans.

But how well had that served her in the past? The bitterness of her brother's loss rolled over her in a fresh wave. Since the day Andrew had come into her life, her grief had subsided a great deal.

She didn't realize until much later that her grief hadn't subsided at all.

CAROL GOODNIGHT

CHAPTER 11

Andrew was such a gentleman. Perfect, charming, easy to talk to, and so handsome, Carolyn thought as she lay on the lounge chair holding hands with her perfect guy.

She tilted her head toward the waning rays of daylight as a cool breeze blew across her skin. Threads of wispy white clouds lingered in the sky, turning orange, pink, and then finally dove grey with hints of chalky mauve.

The hill sloped away beneath them to give a clear view of Century City and the sunset over the ocean beyond. A hummingbird appeared for a few moments to drink nectar from the profusion of flowering pots lining the patio.

Carolyn watched his iridescent feathers change color as he fluttered his wings before zipping to gather with his friends in the tree below. The cheerful chirping melody danced in her thoughts and tuned the song within her that was coming back to life.

"Like another glass of wine?" Andrew asked.

"I'm good." She smiled.

Andrew bent to kiss her.

"I'll bring you one anyway," he said before giving her a quick peck.

As she looked out over the ocean, she thought about how

much her life had changed in the last week.

Andrew always had a ready smile and a strong arm wrapped around her as he paraded her through town like he'd won a contest and she'd been first prize.

"Hon, will you grab a sweater for me, please? I'm getting chilly!" she called in to Andrew. "Hon?"

Andrew didn't answer, so she got up from the lounge chair and walked to the sliding glass door of the master bedroom. She saw Andrew there, bent over, fumbling with something.

She rapped on the window. "Hey sweetie, can you grab my sweater?"

Andrew jerked. His arms tensed as he turned to look at her. His eyes widened and his stare was a cool grey. She saw no sign of life in those vacant eyes. It felt as if he were looking right through her.

Confused, Carolyn wondered what he was doing.

"Andrew?" she called.

Andrew moved his arms behind him as his eyes darted around the room. He saw her sweater on the chair and grabbed it. He looked down at it as he bunched it in a ball. When he looked up again, he was smiling as if nothing had happened.

"I'll be right out with the wine, Dear," he said.

A minute later, he was back with two glasses of wine.

"What were you looking for?" Carolyn asked.

"Huh?" he asked, looking puzzled. He handed her a glass. Carolyn couldn't help but think his smile looked contorted with effort. "What do you mean?"

Carolyn looked at him. Not a shred of acknowledgement appeared on his face.

"Oh. Forgot your sweater. Be right back," he said.

When he returned, he tossed it at her. He seemed pissed off, but Carolyn couldn't imagine why that would be, so she shook her head and let it go.

"So, tell me more about your brother's travels," he said as he held her hand. "I bet he went to all sorts of exotic places."

Carolyn looked at him. An encouraging smile played on his lips.

"You're so thoughtful to ask, Andrew. He spent a lot of time in the middle east." Tears welled in her eyes.

"What did he do there?" he asked.

Even though her brother had shared a few juicy tidbits with her over the years, she knew she could never talk about them. Even to Andrew.

"I'm not sure. Spy stuff," she said, trying to laugh off his question.

"I was an 82nd Airborne Ranger. I'm sure I already know what kind of things he did."

"A ranger?" Carolyn asked. "You never mentioned that before."

Carolyn sat quiet. It didn't jive. For one thing, why would a man from a wealthy family join the military? It isn't unheard of, of course. But it did seem unusual. And second, he didn't carry himself like any of the military men her brother had introduced to her.

"Yep. I did dangerous stuff. Not like those CIA guys with their cushy jobs," he said.

Carolyn lowered her head so Andrew wouldn't see her surprise at his thoughtless words.

Maybe he had been a ranger. And maybe he did do dangerous things. But she didn't like hearing him compare himself to her brother. It sounded like a put-down.

A few minutes later, Andrew announced he had a meeting.

"This late?" she asked.

Andrew smiled at her.

"You don't get rich doing nine-to-five, sweetheart," he said as he walked away.

"When will you be home?" she asked.

Andrew answered with a wave behind him.

Carolyn was asleep when he returned home.

For the next week, Carolyn discovered Andrew's favorite things to eat and did a great job cooking for him. She babied and pampered him, seeing to his slightest need. He seemed to enjoy it.

She was a good listener, too, and empathetic to his life's stories. She tried to comfort him when he would drink too much and complain about his horrible life and childhood. The minor insults he'd suffered seemed blown way out of proportion compared to her own, but she comforted him nonetheless.

Most of his complaints were about women who never loved him enough, treated him horribly, and just used him for his money. Or his parents, who were always trying to control him with money.

She didn't want to judge him and tried hard not to. She'd earned every dime she had and thought it was easier to earn your own way and not have to answer to anyone.

Maybe she wasn't as sensitive as Andrew was. And maybe those small things did bother him. He seemed unable to move beyond his past. He held onto every little complaint.

But she was familiar with the pain of the past and was sure with patience and love he would come to see these slights were only minor.

She tried to give him solace and get him to look at situations from all sides.

That evening Andrew announced he was making dinner.

"You get dressed up. This is a special occasion," he said.

"What's the occasion?" she asked.

"Oh, I don't know. Let's call it an anniversary," he answered.

Carolyn rushed to take a quick shower and slip on his favorite dress. As she passed the front door, she reminded herself to ask him about Dr. Vincent Arpaugh. His mail had come in Andrew's mailbox every day. She thought it might be important so she'd stacked it on the entry table.

But the doctor's mail slipped her mind again as she watched Andrew bustle around the kitchen adding spices and herbs to marinade his dish.

"Still marinating?" she asked as she went to the refrigerator for a piece of cheese.

"NO!" Andrew shouted. "You'll ruin your appetite."

He took the cheese and put it back.

"No cheating," he said as he playfully shook his finger at her.

His phone buzzed and after a quick glance, he said, "I need to get a special bottle of wine." He grabbed his keys.

"Andrew, you have a full wine cellar," Carolyn reminded him.

"Not the right wine," he said.

He winked at her and left.

Carolyn went to the patio to wait.

Two hours later she went to the kitchen and opened the oven.

"It's not even turned on!" she cried.

She opened the fridge and grabbed the cheese. She bit off a chunk as she headed to her room to change. After another hour, she went to bed.

When Andrew arrived home some time later, he was apologetic.

"Andrew, I waited hours," she said.

"I'm so sorry, dear. I'll make it up to you," he said. "I'm really, really sorry.

Carolyn began to realize she'd made a mistake. They should've gotten to know each other before she'd agreed to stay with him. And as particular as he was, she was sure he wasn't accustomed to house guests.

The next morning she woke up late with the odd sensation that Raw Head and Bloody Bones were lurking in Andrew's attic. Andrew had already left for the day, so she tried to shake it off and took a shower to prepare for the day.

As she applied a light powder to her cheeks, she noticed one of her eyeshadow cases was cracked. She picked it up to check, wondering when she'd used it last. She couldn't remember and set it down to check the others. They were all cracked open in the same way.

She made a mental note to buy a more expensive brand for travel as cleaned the counter and stored them in a baggie. Even the small dusting of loose powder stood out on Andrew's gleaming marble countertop.

As she sorted through her clothing, looking for a pink sweater, she stopped. Why did she keep getting that creepy feeling? Everything always seemed tossed around. She found her sweater at the bottom of the stack. She was sure she'd left it on top.

In a dreary region deep down inside of her somewhere, the truth was trying to clarify itself. She ignored it, but she knew something seemed wrong.

I'm losing my mind, she thought as the picture of Andrew rummaging through her garments crossed her mind.

She laughed.

But a pensive crease formed between her eyebrows as she browsed the internet for the next few hours. She knew she'd either have to go home at some point or move.

Living with Andrew was temporary. Maybe it would turn into true love. But who knew what would happen in the future? Carolyn flipped through another listing on the real estate page, thinking it was best to be prepared.

When Andrew came in that evening, he grasped her in his arms and swung her around. After another round of heartfelt apologies for missing dinner the night before, he said, "Guess what! We're going to Las Vegas for New Year's Eve. What do you think about that?"

CHAPTER 12

The plane landed in Las Vegas with a quick bump and a long, drawn-out shimmy. The vibrant energy of Sin City was ramped up more than usual, and everything was shinier and fancier than ever in this shiny, fancy city.

As the bellman opened the door to their room, Carolyn's eyes grew large. The sophisticated neutral palette of cream and white in the stylish, paired with mahogany furniture, was stunning. With one press of the remote control the sheer curtains swayed open allowing the luxurious penthouse suite to overlook the sparkling cityscape and the Las Vegas skyline through floor-to-ceiling windows.

Carolyn gushed in amazement.

The pièce de résistance was a cantilevered pool that extended out from the balcony.

"That looks like fun," she said, hoping there would be a romantic midnight dip.

Andrew looked unimpressed.

"Beige?" he asked, looking at the bellman over the top of his sunglasses before giving him a tip and dismissing him.

He'd been acting as if this celebration was imperative to his business. He'd mentioned his family dynasty and hard work.

Not used to flashy parties, she took particular care with her appearance. She wanted Andrew to be proud of her in front of his friends and business associates.

It'd taken all of her courage to buy the form-fitting velvet gown for the occasion. She'd never worn anything but conservative business suits or jeans and a tee-shirt. The few things she'd bought in New Orleans were the wildest she'd ever owned, and only then because they had nothing plain.

The color of the gown matched the shade of her dark blue eyes. A sheer lace fabric covered the area cut to her belly button with an equally low cut in the back. The velvet hugged her small waist, and while her hip bones protruded because she'd gotten so thin in the last few weeks, the softness of the fabric smoothed them out.

The girl in the shop where she'd bought the gown had said she looked like a beautiful doll.

"Thank you," she said," I'm so nervous."

"Nothing to be nervous about. You'll slay 'em all in that dress!"

Carolyn pulled her long dark hair in an upswept style with wispy bangs and applied an extra thick eyeliner to create a smoky.

She looked in the mirror and was impressed with herself.

"Wow!" she said. "I look stunning."

She walked out of the bedroom as Andrew let in the bellboy with the champagne she'd ordered. She'd wanted to start the evening with a romantic toast.

The bellboy looked up with a startled expression on his face when he saw her. He mouthed the word wow, but glanced at Andrew and lowered his head. He dropped off the tray and left without waiting for a tip.

Carolyn laughed. She wasn't used to that response.

Andrew turned around and glared at her.

"What is so fucking funny?"

Whoa! That sounds familiar. What was with people that didn't like to see people laugh or smile?

"What's the matter, Andrew?" she asked. "Don't you like the dress?"

Andrew scowled.

"Come on," he said.

He led the way as they walked out of the room. He didn't hold the door for her. He didn't walk beside her. He walked in front of her. He didn't hold her hand. He acted as if she wasn't there. He never looked at her in the elevator. He looked at his watch a few times, but never spoke a word. He whisked through the elevator doors and the hotel lobby, knowing she would have a hard time scampering after him in her tight gown and spike heels.

She knew he could hear people commenting on how lovely she looked as they walked by, but for some reason, it seemed to make him angrier.

Four solid, immovable bouncers dressed in custom made tuxedos guarded the entrance of the party venue. Carolyn continued to scamper behind Andrew, but when they arrived at the staircase, he slowed. It wasn't to wait for her. It was to take his time strutting and being seen on his way down to the dance floor.

Strobe lights flashed off and on in rhythm to the throbbing high-energy pop and hip hop mixes. Separating the lavish tiered areas next to the staircase were ceiling to floor diaphanous curtains moving softly with help from a wind machine. The crowd pranced and strutted between the ivory and silver rooms surrounding the dance floor, taking time to stand and pose every few steps.

Andrew walked to the bar overlooking the landscaped patio and then beyond to the strip.

Carolyn caught up to him. She stood in front of him and looked at him questioningly. He didn't acknowledge her at all.

After a moment, he dropped his gaze without changing his expression.

"You have a mouth. Order yourself a damn drink, or don't they teach you that in Podunk? Do I have to take care of everything?"

He walked away from her again and instead of following him, she stood looking after him.

What a dick! She began a slow burn in the hour she sat waiting next to the bar. He never came back, so she headed back to the room to wait for him. Aside from being furious, she was hurt.

"Why would someone treat me this way?" she asked herself. "Who is this man? And what happened to Andrew?"

Once back in the room, she turned on the television and sat staring at it.

Well after midnight Andrew came back to the room. He was drunk and fuming.

He hovered over her, screaming, "How dare you make me look like a fool! I am known in this town! There are important people here! There are movie stars here! You sorry little shit. No one ever walks away from me! Don't you fucking know that by now?"

Carolyn stood up to get away from him.

"What's happened, Andrew?" she asked.

He back handed her in the face. She flew across the room, but before she even hit the ground, she was scrambling back to her feet.

"No one will ever intimidate me again!" she screamed. "I'm not a helpless little girl hiding behind a couch! Not anymore!"

As she tried to get past him, he grabbed her by the neck, pushed her backward, and dragged her to the bedroom. The last thing she remembered was the grimace on his face. His empty cold eyes glared at her with pure hatred while he squeezed her throat.

She was a crumpled mess on the floor when she later regained consciousness. She looked around the room trying to remember what had happened. She slowly moved her arms and legs, making sure nothing was broken. Her neck was stiff, and her throat was sore when she swallowed.

Andrew lay there, almost naked, sleeping in the middle of the king-size bed. Without a sound she gathered her suitcase and bag and crept out of the room. Emptiness and sorrow waved through her. Her slim shoulders heaved with silent sobs as her heart broke yet again.

Thankful it was near dawn with few people milling about the lobby, she ducked into the ladies room in the hotel lobby. She changed into jeans and a "What happens in Vegas" tee-shirt.

She left the beautiful velvet gown laying rolled into a ball at the bottom of the trash can.

Carolyn covered her black eye and the red streaks on her neck with a thick coating of makeup. She pulled on a dark pair of sunglasses, walked out into the bright Vegas morning and hailed a cab. This was the end. The end of Andrew.

Her voice was hoarse, so she tried to speak as little as possible as she flew back to New Orleans to pick up her car. Even with everything at home reminding her of the huge loss of her brother, it would be better than where she'd been. She checked into a large standard hotel near the aquarium. She settled in for a few days of room service and watching TV. No one back home needed to see her bruised neck and black eye.

Andrew called that evening as if nothing happened. She let voice mail pick it up.

"Where are you, Hon?" His message was confusing. How do you smack and choke someone almost to death and then act as if nothing had happened?

As the night wore on, his calls grew more frantic. He sounded desperate, pleading, and ignorant of what happened. Carolyn couldn't believe it.

Around midnight, she answered. He sounded so relieved. He told her he had no recollection of what had happened. He told her an old friend gave him some drug to snort, and he remembered little of the night.

After Carolyn explained what he'd done, he begged, "Oh, please God. Please forgive me. I would never do anything like that on purpose."

"I'm tired and sore, Andrew. I will talk to you tomorrow," she said.

But the next day she turned her phone off, slept, ate, and watched TV. After two more days of messages full of apologies and begging, she agreed to see him. Maybe seeing her battered face and bruised neck would cause him to feel so remorseful he would be willing to make the changes she had been hoping for. She felt they had so much potential together and with some understanding, mostly his, they could have a wonderful relationship.

Andrew flew in that afternoon. Carolyn met him in the lobby and led him to the hotel café. She studied his face as she sat across the table from him. She untied the scarf from around her neck and slipped her sunglasses off while not taking her eyes from his face.

Andrew had no immediate reaction. He looked at her much the way she looked at her car engine when it wasn't working; not knowing what she was looking at, hoping it would be obvious. He was blank. Nothing. Even the room service people had 'a look' when they'd first seen her. In fact, the waitress waiting on them had taken one look at her and then jerked her chin toward Andrew with a scowl.

She had an uneasy feeling it wasn't affecting him. That wasn't even possible, was it?

But then Andrew began his apology. He said all the right things to sound contrite and sorry. It was if he were reading a scripted play. He sounded sincere.

Carolyn listened. Her long-suffering mother had taught her well to be nice. Nice was giving second chances. Nice was letting go of the past and with a positive, non-accusing attitude to persevere toward the future. Nice was looking at tomorrow as a new day and a chance for renewal with a deeper understanding.

Love conquers all. Wasn't that what Aphrodite, the goddess of love, promised?

But the particular love the goddess spoke of, Carolyn remembered later, caused thousands to perish in the Trojan War.

Carolyn was fortunate that she had her brother's influence as well. Her heart grew more protective when she thought of him defending himself when he was so young.

So she listened.

Andrew took a room in the same hotel and for the next few days met her for lunch. She tried hard to give him a chance. It was the 'nice' thing to do.

But on the third, day she found herself sitting in her car at the parking garage, angry and disappointed. Not only had Andrew not paid for parking, he hadn't even arranged for her car to be stored. It was on the schedule for towing the following day.

"I'm sorry," Andrew said. "It's not a big deal. I can buy you ten cars. It's no big deal."

The sunlight flashed on her gold anklet as she pulled her leg into the car and settled herself behind the steering wheel.

"OK, OK, I screwed up. I'll tell you what. To make it up to you, I'll buy you a nicer ankle chain. That one you wear all the time is embarrassing. I'll buy you one with huge diamonds and thick gold," he said.

Carolyn laughed. "Yes, gaudy diamonds and flashy gold would be like you. Your lack of consideration *is* a big deal to me, Andrew," she said. "You only get so many chances in this life, and then it's over. Not everything comes as easy as it does for you. And you can't fix everything with your family's money!"

His once beautiful sky-blue eyes, now empty and frozen, glared at her. A slate gray rim flared around his pupils, likening them to a vulture or a hawk. His menacing look scanned her face as if she were prey.

"You ignorant little bitch! You don't have a fucking clue who I am or what I'm capable of, do you? You are so stupid!" he screamed. His voice rolled over her like lava escaping from his molten heart.

His handsome face contorted from flesh and blood into one of a grotesquely carved animal, granite sharp, hunched-over and leering.

"As far as my chain is concerned, Andrew, it was a gift from my brother," Carolyn said. "A man you could never hope to be. He was honorable and courageous. Not a cowardly bully who snivels and whines when he can't get his way!"

As Carolyn tore away from Andrew's stare, she realized what she'd seen was dark and frightening. And there was something else, too.

Andrew's eyes widened even further. And for a moment, lasting only a brief second, she thought she saw surprise, as if he finally understood something. An epiphany.

With her knees weak and trembling, she put the car in gear, pressed the accelerator, and screeched forward. In the rear view mirror she watched as Andrew stood looking after her. In an instant his shocked, confused expression became the unforgiving, murderous embodiment of evil. The hair on the back of her neck stood up.

It's over!

CAROL GOODNIGHT

CHAPTER 13

As Carolyn looked back, it was easy to see how she'd fallen for Andrew. When thoughts of grief threatened to overwhelm her, he would hold her shaking hands and encourage her to talk about her brother. He never seemed to tire of hearing her stories and asked so many questions about her family. He was so charming and comforting in those early days. He'd made her laugh. Made her forget. Those days hadn't lasted long though. Andrew's own drama became their focus. But in a way, that had been a good thing. It helped distract her from the constant nagging pain of loss. It'd been easy with Andrew always scrabbling for attention.

"Don't think about it!" she told herself. After she'd looked up every single army ranger profile photo on the internet and didn't find him, she knew that had been a lie too. She didn't want to think about how he'd insinuated he was better than her brother.

It was after dark when she left work the second day after arriving home. Weary from trying to keep her mind on work instead of Andrew, she was glad to get home.

Before she reached the door, she noticed one of the sidelights was broken and chunks of glass lay on the stoop.

Carolyn's face washed blank with confusion, as at first glance, the glass looked like cubes of ice.

Every muscle in her body froze, her eyes widened, and for a fraction of a second, her brain couldn't turn fast enough to take in the information.

As she came closer, she noticed scratches around the handle and the broken lock. She pushed open the door to see her television smashed and her leather sofa shredded.

She stepped back out to the sidewalk and called the police.

After the officer cleared the house, she went in to look around.

Everything, from dishes to bed linens, had been tossed.

Carolyn ran to the closet and pushed back the strewn pile of sweaters. She gasped with relief to find her brother's flag was there, even though the frame was smashed as if someone had stomped it.

First her hotel room, now her home. What were the odds? Could Andrew have done this? But why? That was crazy. It couldn't have been him. But the thought it might have been him lingered at the outer edge of her mind.

After filing a police report and two days of cleaning, she went back to her business. Fernando had things running as smoothly as ever. He'd told her the office had been a mess the previous morning. Someone had broken in, but nothing was missing. Only a broken lock.

Not able to keep her mind on anything, she puttzed around, doing the mundane things that needed done. She sat in the red Dodge one-ton in the back lot, taking mileage and thinking about selling the whole thing and moving on.

She used to feel so good about her work. She'd had such a sense of accomplishment when she finished a job. Whenever she'd drive by a renovation project, she'd smile with pride. But now, with her brother gone and her romance, such as it was, over, she felt empty.

A loud thunderclap of noise reverberated from the shop at

the same moment a fiery ball of orange-red flame blasted from the roof. A black column of belching fire and smoke reached high into the sky. The shrill scream of the shop alarm mixed and the muffled roar of the billowing fire hit Carolyn like the shock waves of a mini earthquake. Flames ran from the building to each vehicle in the lot, including the one where she sat dazed.

A blinding burst of flame heated her face as the path of fire flashed to the truck. She jumped into action and jerked the door handle, pushing and pulling up and down as flames engulfed the truck. Singed hair, burnt fuel and rubble dust choked her as the door popped open. Her knees hit the ground with a crack as she tumbled out of the truck.

Hot air burned her lungs as she breathed in the smoking petroleum. Immediate blisters formed on her fingertips from the melted tar as she stumbled to get up on all fours to scramble away. A giant billow of smoke continued to stream out from the center of the building. Glass cracking and splintering wood hissed as ash drifted down, covering the area like black snow in a gremlin nightmare.

Carolyn jumped to get the fire extinguisher, but it was far too late. Flames had engulfed the entire building. Her Thunderbird was already a shell.

"Where's Fernando?"

The last time she'd seen him, he was in the building. She ran half-bent, like a clawless crab, around to the front.

"Oh, thank God," she sighed as saw him sitting on the curb.

There was another explosion.

They both looked around.

"The Dodge," she said to Fernando.

Fernando looked at her through two white spots in the layer of soot covering his face. The tips of his eyebrows and the left side of his hair were covered in ash, giving him the look of an old man.

"What happened, boss?" he asked in confusion.

He held his arm in an unnatural position. His expression, one Carolyn had never seen on the strong young man before, suggested to her that his arm was broken.

"I was on the other side of the building when the thing blew," he said. "I don't have a clue what happened."

Two blaring fire trucks drove through the gates, followed by two police cars. Whiffs of wet rubber mixed with petroleum and burning wood floated over them as the firemen hurried past.

The fire chief stopped to speak with them. He told them there'd be an investigation and after a few cursory questions, he asked one of the policeman to give Carolyn a lift home. Fernando stepped up into the ambulance and sat down on the gurney. Carolyn saw him wince as he laid back. A moment later they raced off, lights flashing, siren screaming, to take him to the hospital. Carolyn called his wife.

She stared out the window from the passenger seat of the squad car at the familiar surroundings. The officer tried to make small talk. She responded with a few "yeses" and "sures."

Everything - the neighborhood, the streets, and her mailbox, all looked the same, but she saw them through different eyes now. Everything was a degree off kilter. She almost missed telling the officer to turn down her street.

Her hands shook as she stood next to the kitchen sink, pouring a glass of rum. She'd kept it for her brother's visits. He used to love his rum and coke. She'd never drunk much before his death, but she was glad it was there now. She popped a Valium, a prescription she'd gotten from the doctor when Mike passed away, and tossed it back with a swig of rum. Ten minutes later, she did it again. She knew it was a deadly combination. She didn't care. Then she stumbled to bed and cried until she exhausted herself to sleep.

She felt exactly the same as before I left. Only now I'm afraid too.

Twelve hours later, the sound of her doorbell woke her from a dead sleep.

When she staggered out of bed, she caught sight of her image in the mirror. She still had soot on her face and her hair looked like Medusa. She pulled it up with an elastic hair band and wet a washcloth in the sink. She was wiping her face as she answered the door. It was the fire chief and a policeman.

"The fire was arson, ma'am, most definitely," the fire marshal said as the two men entered her home.

She had already figured that out. The fact that a stream of gasoline rushed toward each vehicle in the back lot was a dead giveaway.

The questions began, and she hadn't even had her coffee. She offered them coffee and pardoned herself for a minute. She'd never been more thankful for instant coffee in her life. She'd heated a cup of water, tossed in a heaping spoonful of Folgers, and was back answering questions in a minute and fifty seconds.

"Do you know anyone that might have done this?" the officer asked.

Yes, she knew someone.

"Not really," she answered. "I mean, I have an ex-boyfriend, but he's in California."

Even as she wrote his name and address on the report, she didn't think Andrew had done this. He couldn't possibly have been that angry about breaking up.

"I've had a strange sense someone's been following me. My room was ransacked in New Orleans and now here. I've had this creepy feeling since my brother passed away," she said.

One of the officers told her to keep an eye out and if anything else happened, let them know.

Big help, she thought, as they walked out to the squad car.

After they'd gone, she allowed her brain to try to process it.

If Andrew had done it, had he actually meant to kill her, or was he just trying to scare her? Well, if it was the latter, he'd done a damn good job.

She rested on her bed and turned on the TV as she finished her coffee. The more awake she became, the more fearful she was.

When the news flashed a picture of her burning business on the screen, she set her coffee cup down. Her hands were shaking.

I need to get the hell out of here. Now!

After filing the insurance claim and an early morning meeting with a realtor, she packed her bags and loaded them into her Camry. She was happy she'd kept the old beat-up sensible car in case of heavy snow when she'd splurged on the Thunderbird. Mike had teased her for buying the T-bird. Things had been going well for her before his death.

Carolyn's lips pressed together in a straight line as she exhaled.

She thought about Sandy, her next door neighbor when she was a kid. She'd moved to Maine after they'd graduated high school. Sandy's parents divorced when she was in junior high. Her mother had suggested after graduation it was time for her to go live with her father. She'd spent years of trying, with little success, to keep her daughter out of trouble.

Sandy's mom had often complained to Carolyn's mother that Sandy was spirited. That was a polite word for skipping school and drinking all day with the town's known bad boys.

Sandy had been inviting Carolyn to come stay at her a giant old mansion transformed into a bed-and-breakfast for several years now. She'd given Sandy a wide berth for a number of reasons once they started high school. But cheating at games and bumming her baby sitting money for cigarettes didn't seem that important now. Inherited from her father when he passed away, the grounds included cabins spread out over sixty-four acres along the coast of Maine. Carolyn had always thought it sounded boring and isolated. But she couldn't think of any place she would rather be right now.

Sandy's owned a giant old mansion transformed into a bed-and-breakfast. Inherited from her father when he passed away, the grounds included cabins spread out over sixty-four acres along the coast of Maine. Carolyn had always thought it sounded boring and isolated. But she couldn't think of any place she would rather be right now.

Once again, Carolyn found herself running away.

The monotony of the road stretched before her as she settled back into the car seat. She twisted her neck from side to side, stretching and cracking out the tightness. These efforts over the last two hours were paying off. Her mind was clearing and the drone of the highway was comforting.

The car in front of her was only doing sixty-five in the fast lane and the customary long length of cars in the slow lane caused her to press lightly on the brakes to disengage the cruise control. There wasn't much grip. She pressed harder while she waited for a chance to squeeze into the slow lane. All the work stretching her neck was lost.

Her eyes darted from the slow car in front to the slower cars to her right. As the last in the long line of cars passed her, she pulled into the slow lane.

She caught the words "No Northbound Entrance" as she drove under the Thwickingham Village exit sign.

"Oh damn, I'll be stuck out here forever, trying to find my way back to the freeway," she said as she pressed the brakes. Her eyes widened as she waited for them to catch. It took too long. Something was wrong. She drove with caution, her hand on the emergency break until she came to the end of the ramp.

Seeing nothing but corn fields on either side of the rode, she decided to turn right. She stopped at the first service station and asked for the nearest Toyota dealer or mechanic.

"There's one right down the road," replied the girl behind the counter without looking up from her cellphone.

A quarter mile up the road she spotted an old, dirty, hand-painted sign that read: MECHANIC ON DUTY. Carolyn let off the gas and eased the car to a stop close to the pumps. In response to the sound of a customer in his drive, a man whose dirtiness matched the sign sauntered out and gave her a "How do?"

His head cocked to the left, and he was wincing in the sun as he looked her up and down. His face wore about three days growth of a scraggly gray beard while his hair, a grease-slicked black, curled around the top of his balding head, looking somewhat like a wet bird's nest.

"I think my brakes need checked. They feel spongy," she said.

He responded with a huge brown, gap-toothed smile while rocking his biggish head up and down.

"You come to the right place, alrighty. You sure did," he said.

But she wasn't so sure she had come to the right place.

Not sure at all.

She rummaged through her change purse for a few quarters, bought a coke from an ancient coke machine (probably an antique worth lots of money on one of those shows on TV), and sat in an old wooden chair in front of the ancient garage.

A cloud of dust blew around every time someone drove by. She pulled down her sleeves and wiped the top of her coke before she dared to put her lips on it. As she checked around the rim of the bottle top to make sure it was acceptable, she wondered where she'd gotten her penchant for tidiness. Of course, her stepfather was obsessive and controlling about neatness but that couldn't have rubbed off on her.

She brushed that idea out of her mind as she looked around. This place needed a broom, a mop and a few gallons of Windex. No, maybe it just needed a good hosing. No, wait, a power washing. Power wash the entire filthy place. No wait, a bulldozer. There! We have a winner, folks! Give that girl a Kewpie doll.

Where the hell did kewpie doll come from? She tried hard not to think about what spongy brakes might mean.

After examining the car for a few moments the attendant, who she'd named him Festus in her mind, let out a big whistle.

"Woo-hoo!" he yelled. "Come on over here, missy. I gotta show you sumthin."

Carolyn walked over, making sure not to get too close to anything.

"What you got right here is a hole. A hole poked right in your brake line."

Carolyn's stomach dropped.

"Is somebody tryin' to kill you?" He laughed, thinking someone tampering with her brakes inconceivable.

She didn't even fake a laugh in return.

"I can fix it, but it's gonna take a while. You can walk up the road to the resrunt," he said as he pointed his long oil-stained finger up the road.

"My sister works up in there. Tell her I'm a fixin' yer car. She'll give ya some free coffee, on the house."

Carolyn nodded and walked in the direction he'd pointed.

Dust swirled and settled on her sweating body, clinging like a size ten pair of stretch pants on a size fourteen ass by the time she got to the "resrunt." Not one of the old coots driving up and down that old dusty road in their old dirty pickup trucks stopped to ask her if she needed a ride. She wouldn't have taken it, anyway.

But still...

The half-mile walk had given her time to think. She didn't need to wonder any longer if Andrew was trying to kill her. The answer was clear. She'd made the right decision in leaving. Traveling in her own dust cloud, she arrived at the restaurant run by Festus's sister.

Wanda (her actual name) had been the first prize pie maker at the county fair for six years running. Blue ribbons and pie photographs hung everywhere. And rightly so, Carolyn thought, after two giant pieces of cherry pie with ice cream. She closed her eyes and let the sweet, tart cherry taste take her back home.

As good as Mom's, she'd thought before a wave of nostalgia threatened tears. She forced herself to pay close attention to the waitress.

Wanda was a talker as well as a first-rate baker. Her nonstop chatter put Carolyn at ease, and before she realized it, she wasn't shaking. It turned out that Festus's actual name was Earl.

It was hard to imagine that she was sitting here, piling pie and ice cream into her face, when she had just escaped murder. Again. But there was no way Andrew could find her now. She would put her house on the market when she made it to the B&B.

Then what?

She got back on the road after her car was "all fixed up", but she stopped at the next town and pulled into a Holiday Inn. She needed a shower after that afternoon. The room was clean and had a nice view of black cows grazing on a rolling hill. She might as well stay the night.

The drive the next day was uneventful. There was no more pie, but there were a few stops for fuel and a burger from a fast food joint. She listened to the radio, switching back and forth from NPR to top forty pop. She enjoyed the soothing down home stories they told on NPR. It reminded her that things could be normal. She had to turn the pop channel off when songs played that reminded her of the good times with Andrew.

How could I have thought there were any good times? she wondered. How could she have allowed herself to be so fooled? What was the point?

She considered stopping again but decided she might as well use the energy rather than just sit wide awake in a hotel room.

As the car engine hummed along the empty freeway, Carolyn's long auburn hair whipped her face. A haze of thin black clouds stretched across sky, hiding the stars and moonlight as the narrow beam of her headlights lit the path in front of her.

Nighttime had always been a time when frightening possibilities wandered through her mind. But tonight she felt peace.

Gazing straight ahead, only half-aware of her destination, she realized she was alone.

Andrew couldn't bother her. She was safe.

CAROL GOODNIGHT

She took a deep breath and realized that every moment moved her further down the road toward a new life.

CHAPTER 14

Carolyn glanced at the clock on the dashboard when she saw the sign for Cragstone Manor. It was 2:00 a.m.

She drove up the long gravel drive to her friend's imposing, rambling, old mansion, wondering if she were doing the right thing. She shivered as the cold penetrated her entire body. Moonlight cast a ghoulish glow on the mansion, set high on a dramatic headland above Maine's blustering Atlantic Coast.

A beam from the lighthouse a few miles up the road flashed on the uneven gabled roofline, illuminating the steel spires that stabbed the sky. The effect caused them to look as if they'd been struck by lightning. Carolyn looked up at the dark silhouette and then pulled the collar of her sweater tighter around her neck. The shadow of thick serpentine vines, twisted and entangled, crept up the corners of house toward the roof. White splotches of paint clinging to the weathered siding hinted at the house's former prosperity.

A faint yellow light shone through the glass doorway, the only indication that the place wasn't abandoned.

Waves crashed with an uncontrolled and somehow familiar vengeance against the rocks far below. Carolyn stepped up from the gravel driveway to the large flat stones that served as a stairway to the wraparound porch. The rushing wind whipped her hair into a frenzy, cutting her face. A short wooden fence surrounding the front garden caused Carolyn to bend over to unlatch the lock. She almost dropped her travel bag. She let the short door slam shut behind her with a loud creak followed by a quick crack. The occasional flash from the lighthouse helped her keep her bearings while navigating the uneven walkway by moonlight. Skeleton bones came to her mind with every hollow click-clack tap of her heels on the stone.

Dead men tell no tales. She shivered again.

She stopped and followed the searching beam of the lighthouse. The beacon swept over the dark sea, cutting through the mist to guide lost ships home to port. A solitary, isolated guard on vigil through the long night awaiting the first hint of dawn. A kindred spirit. She peeked through the glass door after ringing the bell and saw the night clerk set her book down by the fireplace then come to let her in.

"Hello there, you must be Carolyn. They'll be wicked happy to see ya. They've been expecting you, but not until tomorrow," she said.

"Ayuh, I would've kept the light on for you if I'd known you were coming. Sandy and Peter have already gone off to bed."

"It's quite all right. I'm exhausted," Carolyn answered.

The turn-of-the-century mansion had a stuck-in-time feel, from the old-fashioned wooden cubbyhole mailboxes behind the lobby desk to her narrow room with gaudy floral wallpaper. While grabbing the railing with each labored step the night clerk had given Carolyn a brief history of the place. She explained that Sandy's father had bought the mansion and turned it into a bed-and-breakfast. The former owner, a wealthy ship builder, had built the shingle-style eighteen-room manor with heavy Queen Anne influences in the previous century when the logging industry in Maine was at its zenith. It had served as a home away from home to sea captains from around the world for many years.

"Lucky I was here, Ayuh. This is my last night of the season. We close up for winter. Good thing you came tonight. Tomorrow you'd be sleeping in your car," she laughed. "They're *hard* sleepers."

Carolyn set her travel bag on the bed and thanked her. After the clerk left, she opened the French doors that led out to a small veranda.

After moving a large wing chair in front of the door, she sat watching the waves crest white in the moonlight. The lighthouse's searching beam over the ocean's darkness was hypnotic.

Carolyn reached her arms out into the air, closed her eyes, and breathed. Andrew was far away from her now. The waves dashing against the shore calmed her, and as she drifted off to sleep, the shackles slipped from her soul.

Usually an early riser and busy working by now, it felt good to sleep in. The road trip and the adrenaline rush from the sabotaged brakes were catching up with her. After turning on the little one-cup coffee pot, she stood by the open French doors and looked out to the morning sea. The emerging sun cast a sharp red sheen over the water while clouds tinted mulberry and plum floated like cotton candy from the Euclid Beach Amusement Park she'd visited with her brother as a kid.

"Oh, so I haven't slept that late after all," she said to herself.

She stepped out on the deck then took a quick step back. The house had been built on the edge of the rocks with the deck cantilevered out over the cliff. Covered porches on either side below were separated with a space, leaving her balcony with a straight shot down.

Looking over the edge at high tide, Carolyn could see the drop would be into the sea. She wasn't going out there again until she'd inspected the structure. It was ancient and didn't look safe. She'd seen too many rotten balconies in her day as a construction renovator to trust it.

Flecks of white paint peeled from a charming wrought iron table and chair sitting in the corner between the railing and the back wall. A withered vine stemming from a large clay pot grew up around the railing and entwined itself around the chair back. A long dead flower clung to the chair seat.

No one had sat there for at least a season. She would inspect it from the beach at low tide before she went out there.

The old overstuffed chair in front of the open doors was just what she needed. With her legs tucked under her, she sipped coffee and breathed in the fresh sea air.

She'd dozed off again when she heard a loud argument coming from downstairs. There was a male and a female in an intense argument. She couldn't tell what they were saying.

She ran a brush through her hair and headed down to greet her friend from long ago.

This isolated old mansion seemed an odd place for someone so full of piss and vinegar. She'd heard Sandy married a handsome young sailor from a town not far down the coast. It all sounded so romantic. A gothic mansion on the rocky crags of Maine. Land on the coast, property on a few islands, and a dashing young sailor. It had all the makings of a beautiful love story. *The Wild Girl Settles Down*. She was happy for her friend.

Sandy had been one of the most attractive girls in high school. She ran with a crowd that everyone considered a wild bunch in those days. She'd moved a few doors down from Carolyn the summer before ninth grade, and they became friends by happenstance, not particularly by choice. They rode the bus together, sat in homeroom together, and had gym class together. They knew each other. That's what friendship was comprised of in those days.

Sandy had thought nothing of sneaking out of her bedroom at night and knocking on the window to see if Carolyn would join her. Carolyn was too afraid to try anything so bold as her stepfather might have murdered the entire family as he'd threatened so often, if he'd found her sneaking out at night.

Sandy always had a string of boyfriends that took up most of her time after school. Carolyn loved to hear her tales and share in the shock and giggles from their less adventurous friends, even if she suspected Sandy embellished a big part of it.

She finished dressing and walked down the old creaking staircase toward the smell of fried food. Whatever was cooking, it had her name on it. She was starving. She hoped the stairs would alert them that someone was here. But she heard the argument continue. It got quiet when she knocked on the reception desk. Passing through the swinging doors into the kitchen, she received a shock she hoped hadn't registered on her face.

Sandy's unmistakable light blue eyes flashed with recognition and then darted around the room as if she'd caught her foot in a bear trap. Carolyn wasn't sure why, but Sandy looked disappointed when she saw her.

But for the color of Sandy's eyes, Carolyn might not have even recognized her. Her hooded eye sockets sunk deep, and her stick straight eyebrows tried to arch as her face took on a curious smile. She wiped her mouth on a dishtowel and tossed it over her shoulder before wiping her hands on her threadbare chintz apron.

Once, somewhere in her memory, Carolyn had heard someone refer to the gait of a squirrel drunk on fermented pumpkin as burtzeling. This was how Sandy walked toward her, a dragging shift of each solid leg, making sure she was steady before moving the other.

Carolyn rushed to her and gave her a big hug.

"Long time, no see. How are you?" Carolyn asked her friend.

It didn't take more than a glance to see that the years had taken a toll on poor Sandy. The romantic ideal Carolyn had imagined was her friend's life looked more like rummage sale visits the coast.

Peter, the onetime dashing sailor, stood by the stove, frying round red potatoes in a huge cast iron skillet. He was an imposing man, tall and broad shouldered and carrying a lot of extra weight. Beads of sweat clung to his cheeks. Carolyn hoped that his long straggly hair flowing down to his unkempt beard would stay put and not try to make a guest appearance in the skillet. He had obviously been frying potatoes and lord knows what else by the looks of him, instead of sailing, for a long time. A very long time. Unlike Sandy's awkward smile, Peter's smile carved deep dimple divots in his cheeks. His whole face gleamed with genuine happiness. Or perspiration.

They dined in their huge country kitchen catching up on old times. The back door was wide open to the sea, letting out smoke from a few strips of over-cooked bacon. As Carolyn feasted on fried potatoes, she mentioned nothing about Andrew or her business burning down. She told them she needed a break and thought to look up her old friend.

If you could get past his appearance, Sandy's sailor husband turned out to be a charming fellow. His adeptness in the kitchen went a long way toward explaining his heft.

While Sandy relived her stories about all the good-looking boys she'd bopped in school, her husband grew quiet but continued to eat heartily.

Carolyn steered the subject toward Maine and what interesting things she might try to see. Peter grew animated as he told her that Maine was the lumber capitol of the world in the 1830's. His family had emigrated from Scotland and had found a good living here.

"There was fishing, granite quarrying, textile mills, and shipbuilding. In fact, the fellow who built this very house was a shipbuilder. Money was easy in those days, but those days are over now," he said.

"By the turn of the century, the waters were over-fished, and the saw mills couldn't compete with the larger forests out west. Maine went from a few bustling industries to a quiet backwater."

Peter, his father, and grandfather before him had made a decent living with fishing, he told her, but times had changed. Maine's rustic, undeveloped land had great appeal to vacationers and became a summer cottage destination.

"The best you can do nowadays is to own a quiet vacation get-away or a trendy chic restaurant that caters to folks needing a break from the city," he said.

He grew breathless reciting the information and paused for a moment.

There were two paths to explore he explained when he had caught his breath. She could hike along the coast and climb down to check out the tidal pools or walk through the meadow that led through the blueberry barrens and into the forest. He warned her to leave before the tide came in and not turn her back on the waves if she took the coast hike.

"You need to skedaddle when the ocean begins to surge into the pools."

She could tell he had spent many hours exploring the area himself. His eyes lit up while talking about the coast. Boating and fishing had been his life before he met Sandy and she had convinced him to help her run the B&B and her other property.

"I love it though and would do anything to help my lady," he said, looking over at her with affection.

Sandy laughed. "You're a worthless piece of shit that wouldn't know the meaning of love if it jumped right up out of the bowels of hell and bit you in the balls."

Then she looked at Carolyn and nodded as if to confirm she had set him straight. He dropped his head, got up, and walked out the kitchen door. Sandy asked her if she wanted a scrumptious blueberry muffin and if she had ever heard anything about Eddie Harris, the cute boy who lived around the corner when they were in school.

This is definitely not the romance I had pictured, thought Carolyn.

Relieved to get away from the house, she gathered her flying hair into a ponytail and then tightened up the lace on her hood. Walking along the top of the steep bluff in the strong updraft, she felt as if she might lift up and fly. A massive blueberry field of every imaginable shade of red, orange, brown, and green undulated toward the edge of the forest along the coastal path. Carolyn startled a fox feasting on wild berries. She stood still, watching him until he scampered away.

The changing hues of fall covered the red oak, maple, and birch trees on the forest path and lower slopes, putting on a magnificent final show before winter set in. She caught a whiff of the damp earthiness of walnuts between the short gusts of sea air.

The house became a shadow peeking through the misted fog that wafted off the sea. The weathered gray shingles blending with the granite outcroppings on the cliff matched in color. It made for a hazy horror story kind of setting. Four monumental chimneys loomed above the differing levels of slate roofing, with only a faint wisp of smoke from one fireplace blowing inland and blending with the fog. Carolyn noticed, for the first time, the narrow square tower rising above the mansion on the farthest side away from her. The tower opened onto a tiny cupola platform with a decorative spindle railing.

A widow's walk.

There was a romantic tale, told so often along the coast, about the platform used by the wives of sailors. They stood watching out over the ocean for the return of their husbands. The watch was often in vain as the ocean was a fickle master. With many seamen never to return, it left their widows walking the small deck and grieving. The thought of the loneliness and the constant state of wondering made Carolyn think about her brother. As an effort to avoid breaking down, her mind jumped to Andrew.

She asked herself the same thing over and over. Why would he try to kill her? She'd start at the beginning and go over their conversations in her head.

She kept reviewing the experience, and each time she came to the swamp, she'd stop. She could never move beyond that point without immediately jumping to the explosion.

She shook her head, trying to make it all straight.

A steep, rocky trail cut back and forth into the cliff, serving as rugged stair steps down to the sea. The first step was the hardest to navigate; it easily measured the depth of two or three feet. A lone woodpecker hammering away in the nearby forest sent an eerie knocking sound echoing through the fog. Climbing down to the shore was steep and Carolyn was glad she'd worn good tennis shoes. She couldn't ever imagine Sandy climbing down here. The thought of Sandy navigating these rocks struck her as funny, and she laughed aloud for the first time since her workshop had exploded.

She was sure it had been a long time since Sandy's husband, Peter, had climbed down here as well. Grabbing large tree roots growing from the side of the cliff kept her from slipping all the way down in one swift bump and slide.

Coming back up would be harder but not as scary because she would be looking up. She stepped off the last rock and walked to the water to rinse her muddy hands. Quarter-size round stones of every earth tone color composed the rocky shoreline. Set back from shore, boulders lay across the glacier-hewn stretches of large granite slabs. Darting back and forth with the waves, Carolyn headed over to see if she could find any foundation problems under the old house from the cliff side. She was never comfortable sitting on a balcony without checking the structure underneath. She'd heard of too many balconies falling off, especially on vacation properties. This one hung over the edge of a cliff, so it had farther to fall than most. The shore narrowed as she walked toward the underside of the mansion.

The massiveness of Cragstone Manor, hidden from the front approach to the house, revealed its broadest facade in the back, facing out into the ocean. Carolyn guessed the ship captain had built the house this way, not only to allow for the view, but also to commandeer cool sea breezes into the house.

Large overhanging eves extended over two expansive porches from around each side of the house on the first floor. The paint on the balustrades had worn so thin it looked like a whitewash, or rather gray wash. Dirty small-paned window sashes looking like the many black eyes of an insect hung above the newer large plate glass windows on the third floor. Carolyn spotted the balcony of her room. It was placed in the exact center back of the house, right above the separation between the two wrap around decks.

After satisfying herself there were no obvious structural problems visible from below, she sat down to rest on a rock. Knobs of granite covered in rockweed formed a myriad of ledges, making perfect tidal pools. She was soon on her hands and knees, mesmerized by the tiny world. Two crabs raced past a slow-moving starfish making his way toward a cluster of tiny snail eggs dangling on the edge of one rock. The fringed siphons of several mussels with their shells open fanned themselves while barnacles combed the water with their rake-like mouths looking for food. Adding color to the pond were flat, delicate sea lettuces and wispy red fronds that swayed while sea urchins grazed through them. A few small clams drew seawater into their bodies, straining out tiny particles of nutrition, while a crab next to them was carefully stalking its prey. Tiny shrimp-like scavengers zipped through the shallow water. Their relentless search and devour movements reminded her of Andrew.

Carolyn sat back on the rock seat, pushing thoughts of her shop's explosion out of her mind, and checked the field guide she'd found in her room. She tried to identify a few creatures. Gazing at the pool, she wondered if the police had any news on the investigation. She knew they'd find no clues and probably never would. She knew enough about Andrew to know he would never be held accountable for anything.

A wave washed over her shoes and she turned around to see the tide coming in fast. She remembered now that she was not supposed to turn her back on the sea.

Lost in the tiny pool and in her large mystery, she'd forgotten about the tide coming in. Running back to the path, she slipped on the first step and scraped her shin. She was about halfway up the steep climb when the field guide, crammed in her pocket, fell out and bounced down the steps she had climbed.

"Oh, the hell with it," she said. "I'll buy Sandy another one. I am not going back down to get that."

She grabbed at tree branches to gain footing on the rocks and was making it fairly well when the rain started. The rocks were slick and hard to navigate going down, but the wet muddy rocks coming back up were nearly impossible. Almost at the top, she spotted Sandy's husband, Peter, ambling toward her in the heavy rain.

Thank God!

She knew that last large step up the muddy cliff would be harder than the previous twenty minutes climbing on all fours.

Peter reached down, grabbing her hand and the back of her jacket, and hoisted her up over the ledge.

"You should've been watching the sky. Didn't you see it coming?" he asked in a concerned but admonishing tone.

She looked out through the rain to see an enormous circular shelf of black cloud off shore. The thick, low, horizontal rushing monster was heading their way. As the gusty front hit the shore, the cloud seemed to rise, exposing the belly of the storm, still off in the sea, as a turbulent roiling gale storm. Dark shafts of heavy rain extended from the low dark cloud into the black sea. A sudden shift in the wind caused a strong downdraft that knocked them to their knees.

She was grateful Peter had shown up when he did, and a little embarrassed that she had not paid more attention, especially after he'd warned her. Carolyn sensed the softness in his reprimand though. This was what actual concern sounded like. Not the robotic words Andrew used toward the end.

The dark shaft of rain and hail hit them, then and Carolyn forgot all about Andrew. By the time they made it to the house, the heavy rain had washed off most of the mud. As they headed around the back, Peter said, "Please take your shoes off and leave them here, under the overhang."

He'd said it in such a way it gave her the impression they would both suffer if she didn't do that. She took off her soaking wet jacket and left it outside, too. Up in her room, after peeling off her cold clothes and then underwear and bra, she took a long hot shower. She put on some sweat pants and a heavy sweater. When she came out of the bathroom, she noticed a pot of hot tea on the table next to the chair she'd moved in front of the French doors. She knew Peter must have brought it and was touched, but also glad that she'd lingered in the shower.

She sat into the evening, sipping the tea long after it had gone cold. The shrill voice of her friend Sandy sounded on and on into the night. She wondered if it was like this all the time or more so now that all the guests were gone for the season.

The next morning, she tiptoed to the kitchen, knowing Peter and Sandy weren't awake yet, and grabbing a piece of toast, she slipped on her wet tennis shoes and went for a walk outside. After pouring down all night, the rain had slowed to a drizzle. . Carolyn thought about the arguing the night before and wondered if she would not be able to hear it if she sat on the veranda this evening.

The Victorian style gardens around the house had fallen into an overgrown jumble of large ornate plantings combined with weeds. She wondered how many years of neglect it would take to get in this shape. Peter's talent lay in cooking, not gardening. She wondered, what, if any skill Sandy had. She was all too familiar with people whose only talent was inheriting well. Andrew came to her mind again. She realized she was doing the same thing with Sandy that she'd done with Andrew. She was using her to distract herself from a terrible reality.

Perhaps inheriting well was Sandy's talent, as it was with Andrew, Carolyn thought, trying to shove Andrew's memory back in the dark where it belonged.

She squeezed around the back side of the house. It had been built a yard, at most, from the edge. Despite the age and neglect of the old place, it looked to be in sturdy shape. However, that evening she still couldn't bring herself to sit outside on that veranda.

The next day, after another evening of Cragstone Manor's

basic entertainment - a great hearty fried meal, digs at Peter, and listening to arguments late into the night, she took the ferry to the island where Sandy owned a few summer cottages. She'd had enough of reminiscing with her old friend. Sandy had given her the key, and if the place were satisfactory, she would spend the winter out there. She wanted to be by herself. Not a single person came to mind with whom she wanted to spend any time.

CAROL GOODNIGHT

CHAPTER 15

Carolyn had been on small passenger ferries before, but this was the first time she'd driven a car on one. It seemed strange. But the people here did it every day.

There were three teens with backpacks and a mom with two younger children who must have been on their way to school.

I wonder how often school closes due to weather, she wondered.

When they were about three quarters of a mile away from shore, she could see Cragstone Manor hovering over the cliff's edge. The outlines of the roof and widow walk were the only giveaway it was a building and not another rock outcrop. In the fog and drizzle the mansion looked as harsh and foreboding as the cliff.

Her short drive through flaming red grasses that grew where patches of soil clung to the rock slab island seemed promising. After the general store, she hadn't seen even a single sign of another living soul.

At a high spot in the road the cottage at the end of the island came into view. It was a short, stout, square structure. Hand hewn, weathered gray cedar shakes covered the roof while a lighter brown shingle covered the exterior walls. Scavenged rocks from the area made up the back stair steps and the foundation as well. The window and door trim and the deck in the front and the Adirondack chairs looked as if they'd had a fresh coat of white paint.

It wasn't as old as the B&B, and it looked as if Sandy's husband maintained it well. Much better than the mansion. Sandy probably made more money on it as a summer rental than she did at the B&B. Lord knows, if she treated her guests anything like she'd treated Carolyn, no one would ever stay there.

Surrounding the quaint cottage was a meadow filled with the last gasp of blooming wild flowers. Fading purple lupines stretched from the driveway entrance to the edge of the rocky beach. Hollyhocks in muted dusty shades of cream and pink lined up next to the house, bent over in a curtsy as if greeting their queen. The three-acre secluded ocean front property, as advertised in the brochure, was a wonderful setting for birders because of its proximity to the wildlife preserve that made up several adjacent islands.

A small red canoe lay resting on its side and tied to a post next to the rocky beachfront about thirty feet from the front door. Carolyn walked to the water's edge. She sat in one of the four Adirondack chairs surrounding a fire pit.

It was the perfect place for roasting marshmallows, but best of all, there were no neighbors.

Sandy had warned her that this was the only cottage on this edge of the island. Most of the island people lived fifteen minutes up the road, close to the general store. She'd said the population on the island was only forty to forty-five in the winter and only a few dozen more in the summer.

Carolyn was surprised when she opened the door and stepped inside. Where the old Victorian B&B was dark and depressing, the cottage was bright and cheerful.

Bleached white-oak tongue-in-groove paneling covered the high post-and-beam cathedral ceiling and walls. The cabinets in the kitchen were a soft cream color and most of the furnishings wore matching slipcovers. Two wing chairs sat angled in front of the large stone fireplace masoned with various sizes of round smooth rocks taken from the property. She admired that. None of that prefab half-inch fake rock that fireplaces were made of these days.

Very nice. Her approval echoed when she saw the three cords of wood stacked outside next to the subservient hollyhocks.

The French doors in the bedroom opened to the back deck, looking out over the sea and brightening the cheerful room even more.

She jumped on the thick feather bed on the mattress and pulled a pastel flower quilt over herself.

As she sunk down into the bed, she sighed, "Yes! This will do nicely."

After unpacking, she headed back to the store. The storekeeper was surprised to see her.

"I haven't heard word one about Sandy renting the beachfront for the winter," she said. "Far as I knew, she only rented the one on the other side. Do you know what winter is like in Maine? On the island?" the shopkeeper asked. She smiled but Carolyn noted the skepticism in her voice.

"No, but I guess I'll find out." Carolyn laughed.

"Do you need any groceries ordered from the Main?" the shopkeeper asked. "I usually keep the standard stuff here, but I can special order if you need anything."

Carolyn pulled out the loose bills wadded up in the bottom of her purse to pay for her groceries. She fumbled with a lone credit. A confused look crossed her face as she wondered why finding the credit card bothered her as she smoothed out the cash. When she noticed the shopkeeper eying her, she shoved it back in and forgot about it.

Her shoulders relaxed and a sense of relief filled her mind as she drove back over the isolated island to her new home. She'd been fighting thoughts of Andrew but when she looked out over the dark surface of the ocean, she remembered that sweltering day in the bayou. A cold shiver crept up her back and her neck hunched back in the seat.

"Later," she said. "I'll think about it later."

Peter had mentioned the television service on the island was sketchy at best, so she'd stopped at a used bookstore and bought a box of paperbacks before hopping the ferry. She loved the old southern lawyer stories by John Grisham and dozed off in one of the wing chairs by the fireplace, dreaming of swaying palm fronds and chirping cicadas. A brisk gust of wind popped open the window and a chilly breeze blew across her skin followed by a ripple of goose bumps.

She wondered how long she'd been sleeping as she reached in her purse to check the time on her phone.

"Hmm, not there," she said.

It wasn't in her suitcase either. Then she remembered she'd left it plugged into the charger at Cragstone Manor in the small phone purse.

She'd have to get it the next time she was over on the Main, as the shopkeeper at the little grocery called the mainland. There no one she wanted to talk to anyway. Good thing she'd had cash, she remembered, as her credit cards were in her phone purse.

Then realization set in. She was unreachable.

After enjoying that fact for a few minutes, she had another realization. She couldn't call for help. She reached in her purse and flattened out the rest of the bills she had crumpled in the bottom of her purse. Twenty-three dollars. Then she remembered why finding the credit card bothered her. She'd left the rest of her credit cards in her phone purse.

At least she had one, she thought. Maybe she'd to go back tomorrow.

The next week she spent taking long walks on the shore, reading in the feather bed, and sleeping. She was catching up on lost peacefulness and forgot about her phone.

CAROL GOODNIGHT

Toward the end of her time with Andrew, she hadn't realized how on edge she'd been. No matter how hard she tried not to think about him, her thoughts would wind back around to him. Had he ever loved her? How could he want to kill her because she wanted to get away from him? She feared him. And who was the big guy?

She asked herself these questions, and more, every day and night. After a while, though, the nagging questions died down and she put it out of her mind. She was either breathing in the brisk Maine air or lost in the pages of a mystery based in the Deep South.

While lost in thought on an early morning beach walk, she heard the crunch of stones and turned to see someone running up behind her. She hadn't seen anyone out here before. In fact, she'd only seen a few people at the store once or twice.

The guy running toward her held a wire contraption up over his head. The thing looked as if it could be some sort of old-time TV antennae.

She darted her head around. Only a churlish shore to one side and an open field on the other. She was alone and wondered how she hadn't realized how vulnerable she was before this.

The man with the strange contraption yelled as he came closer. "Did you see her? Did you see her?"

Carolyn's eyes were still searching the landscape for cover as she answered. "Who?"

"That Rustie! She flew right by here! You had to see her! How could you miss her?"

Carolyn took a breath as she realized he was talking about a bird.

"She went that way," she said, pointing into the meadow of dead lupines behind her cottage. "She landed near that bush with the red berries."

As the man ran up past the house, the bird flew up and out over the ocean toward the neighboring island.

"Ah crap," he said, as he walked back toward Carolyn with the wire thing hanging at his side.

"Hi, I'm Dean. That was a female Rusty Blackbird. She's on the endangered list and I'm trying to find out more about her migratory patterns. I've been studying her all summer on the reserve over there." He pointed to the nearby island.

"But she's been over here since early fall. I'm sure she's ready to migrate, but I'll stay here all winter to see how long she stays."

"Oh," said Carolyn.

"See ya later," he said. He took off and Carolyn watched him trot around the end of the island and out of sight.

Carolyn shrugged her shoulders. "Hmm, that was weird."

There was a chill in the air that evening as winter closed in, so she lit a small fire in the fire pit next to the shore. On her lap was a bag of marshmallows that had come in with her supply order the day before. She was sharpening a stick when she saw Dean walking around the end of the island and head her way. He was carrying two cans of beer. He handed one to her and popped open the other as he sat down.

"Oh, marshmallows, mmm," he said.

She popped open her can and introduced herself as she held it up toward him.

"Hi. I'm Carolyn. Nice to meet you Dean, the bird guy," she said.

He laughed. "Actually, everyone who knows me knows my true love is turtles."

"So, are you cheating on your true love with the rustie?" She smiled at her own joke.

Dean the bird guy kept her entertained until dusk. They'd found they'd both started out at Sandy's B&B and had decided to rent a cabin on the island. His reason was to study birds. Carolyn didn't mention her reason.

Dean had loved animals his entire life, he told her. He felt lucky to get on this project trying to protect the Rusty Blackbirds. He told her of his travels around the world, starting with how he'd taken the train around Europe and visited all the old zoos. He'd also volunteered to build crates in Hawaii to send breeding pairs of endangered birds around the globe. He mentioned he was captain or sergeant at arms, she couldn't remember which, of the Fairy Bluebird breeding book.

She wondered if that was considered bird porn while he explained his last adventure. He had participated in the captive breeding program on the island of Rota. Snakes brought in on the wheels of airplanes in Guam had bred well and eaten all the bird eggs. They tried to replenish the birds by raising them on nearby islands then reintroducing them to their native land.

"Why didn't they kill the snakes?" Carolyn asked.

"They do," he said and then continued telling her more about his many trips to Africa. He talked about particular animals as if they were great old friends. By the end of the evening, she was sure some of those animals were old friends of his.

Dean told her he'd rented the cabin on the windward side of the island. He mentioned that the couple who had rented him the cabin were hard-core arguers, and she laughed, remembering Sandy and Peter. With that they both looked over to the Main and could make out a small light at Cragstone Manor.

"I went to high school with Sandy," Carolyn said. "Don't hold it against me."

They both laughed.

Dean pulled two more cans of beer out of his jacket pocket, and when they'd finished those he said he'd better be getting back home.

"Five a.m. comes mighty early around here," he said.

Carolyn never got around to roasting the marshmallows. They didn't sound appetizing after she'd tasted the beer. And although she rarely drank, the beer tasted good and she slept well that night.

Fall quietly snuck out one night as winter marched in and blanketed the island with snow. Vicious freezing winds blowing across the cold sea kept her inside the cottage. She rarely even opened the door, except to get wood for the fire. Carolyn liked that just fine. She had seen no one except Dean in over three weeks. And she'd only seen him walking down the beach with his wire thing held up in the air after dawn on two mornings. She'd already read half of the books in her box and still hadn't tired of sitting in the wing chair in front of the fireplace reading or falling asleep in the feather bed. She'd added a few more quilts to the bed, so only her nose was chilly when she slept.

After not speaking to him in weeks, Dean knocked on her door one night after dusk. He pointed across to the Main toward Cragstone Manor. There were unmistakable lights of an ambulance blinking. He came in, shook off the snow, and while she heated water for tea, they pondered over what might have happened.

Dean thought Peter had gotten fed up with the bitching and socked her one.

"Right in the face. Pow!" He gestured an uppercut. "That would shut her up for a few days."

Carolyn giggled and then wondered aloud if Peter might have had a heart attack.

"He ate all that fried food and was carrying a lot of extra weight."

"Poundage," Dean replied. "The man had some poundage going for him."

Carolyn felt sorry for whatever had happened to either of them. She would go to the general store tomorrow and see if there was any news.

The next morning just after nine, she forged her way through the snow to scrape her car. Even with her mittens and heavy winter coat, she could feel the wind blow through to her skin. There was a layer of hard ice underneath the fluffy snow. Her fingers grew so cold they had no feeling by the time she finished.

The car started right up and helped with the defrosting but

that only succeeded in making the misery a slight bit more bearable. She hoped the unplowed road was passable after all of this. By the time she made it to the store, her fingers were frozen into place. Not by the cold, but by gripping the steering wheel so tight that they had become stiff. The road was as slick as an ice skating rink after a Zamboni polish. She had a hard time with the door handle to the store and ended up using both hands to finagle it open.

She recognized several people from previous trips to the store. But she'd never seen the three standing around the counter.

"It's a hell of a thing," said the shopkeeper. "I knew that old house would kill her one day."

"What happened?" Carolyn asked.

"She was out on a balcony and it fell off. She went straight down, all the way," replied the shopkeeper.

"Peter must have gotten tired of being cooped up with her nagging all winter and pushed her out," said one old guy who Carolyn had never seen before.

"I'd think that too if I hadn't seen him with my own two eyes fixing that old hot water heater in the rental next to the grocery all day," the shopkeeper replied.

"He never was too good with tools," said one red-haired lady.

"She was pretty bashed up, I heard. Lay there a long time until Peter got home and went looking for her," said the shopkeeper

"I hear he's beside himself," said another person she'd never seen before.

"The squad had a hell of a time getting the body back up that cliff," said the shopkeeper.

Carolyn couldn't take anymore. She stepped outside for a few minutes, but soon the cold got the better of her and she went back in. Everyone was quiet. They must have heard she was a childhood friend.

Forty-five minutes later Carolyn was on the ferry. She stood next to the snack bar, the warmest place on the boat, and sipped coffee while trying to warm her hands and still the shudder growing inside her. She knew it wasn't from the cold.

There was nothing wrong with any of the balconies on that old place. She'd inspected them. What could have happened? Maybe the cliff gave way and undermined the structure? But that seemed unlikely since the cliff was granite.

But it could happen, she supposed. Her face wrinkled in doubt.

She dreaded seeing Peter. She'd been having a hard time with her own grief since she'd lost her brother. It was unbearable watching someone else suffer it.

She was glad she had come though. Peter ran to her, bent over, and cried on her shoulder.

"I'm so glad to see you," he said. "You loved her too. Oh god. How am I going to live without her?"

His love for her moved Carolyn. Sandy had been awful to him for years. She was actually a downright bitch and Carolyn didn't even like her. But she was gone now.

"Rest in peace, my dear, sweet Sandy," Peter kept saying.

When he stopped sobbing, he wanted to talk about the horror he'd experienced. Carolyn didn't want to hear it, but he had been kind to her, and he needed her right now. So they sat down in the kitchen and she started the fire on the stove to make tea.

"When I came home, all the lights were all off," he started.

"It was weird. Except for the light in the room you stayed in Carolyn. That light was on."

Carolyn's eyes widened and she stopped breathing for a moment.

"I called for her. 'Sandy? I'm home!' It was my Ricky Ricardo greeting." He paused and looked into space as if he could see the past. "She loved that."

Carolyn could imagine Sandy rolling her eyes every time he said it, but she nodded, still trying to grasp the relevance of her room's light being on. Her skin prickled with goose-bumps.

"I felt the draft from the open French doors before I even got to the top of the stairs. When I got to the room, the French doors were standing wide open. The railing was gone. I ran down the stairs and grabbed the flashlight from the back porch. I kept shining it over the edge. I saw her lying down there. Her body was so twisted and bent up," he said as he began sobbing again.

"The police were here all night. I'm exhausted." He slumped his shoulders.

Carolyn made him drink a few sips of tea and take a Valium. She had been carrying a prescription of it everywhere with her since her brother died, just in case. And sometimes, like now, it came in handy. She walked with him to his room and helped him plop into the big empty bed.

She felt bad for him. The worst was yet to come. The empty days and nights, the random thoughts and memories, the constant heartache. Yes, it was all ahead of him.

"They found your purse with your phone and credit cards strewn around on the balcony, Carolyn," he said right before he drifted off.

A shock wave began at the base of her spine and bubbled up to her scalp. Her hair stood on end and her world became silent.

What did that mean? Why would she take my purse out on the balcony?

CHAPTER 16

Carolyn stood outside on the cold deck of the ferry for the return trip to the island. The wind howled in a low whistle as it whipped over the waves. The penetrating blasts tossed her hair, whipping it against her face as she tried to clear her head.

Not much stopped these hearty Maine folk from their routines of life. The ferry cruised back and forth every day, only missing those few days when a big storm blew in. As far as Carolyn was concerned, the entire winter had been the "big" storm.

She enjoyed being alone, but if she'd needed to get out in the weather, she don't think she could've handled it. She cupped the instant coffee from the ferry snack bar in her hands for warmth and took a sip.

She pitied Peter. It didn't help that he didn't have many friends as no one ever wanted to be around Sandy. He'd have to start another life.

She stared at the old house through the mist until thick fingers of fog hid it between their grip. As the rotting posts of the pier disappeared in the dark shadows, she lowered her head. Just as well she couldn't see it, she thought.

She pulled her phone from her bag to check the messages.

CAROL GOODNIGHT

No frantic calls or texts from Andrew. No threats.

But there were several notices from the bank. Carolyn felt relieved. Perhaps the growing suspicion that Andrew had something to do with Sandy's death was in her imagination.

Her relief was short-lived however, when she found that her personal and business accounts had been shut down due to lack of funds and excessive overdrafts.

Carolyn closed her eyes. Andrew was a thief. A con. It made sense now. He lived off women.

The mail with someone else's name at the house in Hollywood hills made sense. The supposed family plantation that he hadn't bothered to inspect made sense. Even his anger made sense. Carolyn was comfortable, but by no means wealthy. He was likely upset he'd wasted so much time for such a paltry payday.

Fortunately she'd lagged in turning in her insurance paperwork for her destroyed business and the sale of her home hadn't been finalized.

Still, she seethed when she mentally added up the amount of money he'd stolen. A lifetime of work. Stolen! And he'd covered his tracks well. There would be no retribution.

She flipped through her phone and found the number of her brother's military pal that had arranged the funeral. He'd been so kind.

"Anything you need, Carolyn." She remembered Oscar saying.

Before she reached the dock he called her back with information.

"Of course I'm not permitted to release personnel records. Especially from another branch. But what the hey. I'm out next week. And I owe your brother a solid. He was my best drinking bud when he was stateside. The times we had! God, I miss him. How are you holding up?"

Carolyn pinched her lips in a thin line before answering.

After a few moments of small talk that sounded hollow and lame even to herself, Oscar chimed in.

"Anyway Carolyn, I have the file. This is a bad guy you're dealing with. I implore you to stay away from him. He's not 82nd airborne. He's nothing. Worse than nothing. He did 10 weeks of basic training for the national guard and then was designated UNSAT for unsatisfactory participation. The clown only reported for three weekend drills. In the old days jerks like this were hung for desertion."

After a pause he said, "I'm sorry Carolyn. Step away from this man. Things have a way of coming full term. And you do not want to be around when his karma comes calling. Where are you?"

After Carolyn explained she'd been checking Andrew's record for a friend, she thanked him and assured him that she was doing well. The concern in his voice eased a bit when she said she was in Maine on an extended holiday. It sounded as if he were rustling papers and busy with people in his office but she forged on.

"Was he court-martialed?"

"No. It takes a lot of paperwork over a six month period to opt these wastes out. The army has already invested enough time and energy trying to make them men. They usually push them off the books.

Carolyn was silent as she fought off tears of frustration.

"Maybe I can rustle things up a little before I go," he said.

Carolyn hoped this meant he would cause Andrew at least a small measure of inconvenience.

She thanked him again for arranging the funeral ceremony and said goodbye. As she hung up she heard him call her name to say something else. She knew her voice would crack if she said one more word. If he called back, she wouldn't answer. She was too ashamed. She'd fallen for a conman who was not only a thief, but a coward.

The trickle of tears itched a trail under her scarf as she pulled into the driveway of her cottage. While she put the car in park and scratched her neck, she eyed the cracked-open back door. Her jaw tightened as she stepped out of the car, all the while fighting the impulse to get back in and drive away. Her heart throbbed in fear as the cold, wet wind gusted around the cottage. It chilled her to the bone. With each slow footstep toward the house, every fiber of her being commanded her to run the other way.

"Run!" Dean yelled as he came tearing around the corner.

She was close enough to see that his right eye was swollen shut and his arm hung twisted at an awkward angle. Behind him a giant man took a swipe at the back of his head. It threw Dean into the railing and caused him to roll against the porch.

Carolyn's mind shot to full speed. All the experience with escape plans she'd made as a child kicked in. She knew she couldn't get off the island before the guy caught up with her. If she tried to take the ferry, he could kill her before anyone realized what was going on.

She also knew who had sent him. The phone on the balcony at Cragstone manor made sense. Andrew must have used it as a GPS. She wondered why he'd waited so long to catch up with her, and why he'd killed Sandy. Maybe she wouldn't cooperate and tell him where she was?

"Run!" Dean screamed again.

Carolyn instinctively did as Dean commanded. She ran to the canoe, slipped the rope off the post, dragged it the few feet to the water, and pushed it off hard. She jumped in at the last second. The force from the push took her out about six feet. She jerked the paddle back and forth to release it from the holder and smashed it into the water. Paddling first right, then left, she dug into the water as fast as she could. When she was fifteen feet from shore, she turned to look back. The big guy was bent, standing at the edge with his hands on his knees, gasping.

Those big guys weren't much for running, she thought as something about him caught her eye. She looked closer at the heaving giant on the shore. A hot feeling warmed her body as she realized she'd seen this man before. Her eyes narrowed in concentration.

Dean limped around the side of the cottage and Carolyn turned her attention to his hunched figure. She hoped he'd be all right. All he ever wanted to do was mind his own damned animal business. He was as much of a loner as she was trying to be.

She took a breath and positioned the paddle.

After she'd rowed out of sight to the other side of the sanctuary island, she stopped and rested the paddle on her knees.

The man she thought she'd once loved had lied about his military service. He was no better than a deserter. That stung considering all her brother had given. And he'd stolen from her. But worst of all, he'd had her friend killed while trying to kill her.

Darkness overwhelmed Carolyn and her shoulders wracked with sobs as she thought about Sandy and Peter. She sobbed for a long time before her deep gasps grew calm. She'd been in this place in her mind before. It felt like strength. After the tears, came a new resolve. A compulsion to move forward. A need to keep moving or sink.

She was sure if Andrew were here right now she could strangle him with her bare hands and row away without another thought. But he wasn't here. Like a coward, he'd sent a giant man to kill her.

She pushed off and rowed with a new determination toward the ferry terminal. At the edge of the small cove before the bay, she rowed up to shore. She hopped out and dragged the canoe a few feet up the bank.

She crouched down to watch. It was freezing but she didn't feel cold. The burn from within kept her warm.

She watched the big guy drive up to the dock and onto the ferry. The giant man in the economy rental car was hard to miss. The man stepped to the railing and stood with the wind to his back while trying to button his thin overcoat.

She was sure he wasn't a local. Must have flown in from L.A. As he talked into his phone, she could see his hand gesturing back and forth in a heated conversation. When he hung up he looked down and shook his head. She knew he had been talking to Andrew. She'd felt the exact same way in New Orleans when she'd ended the conversation with him.

Carolyn's fingers were numb as she pushed the canoe back in the water. She rowed back to the cottage, retrieved her purse from the car, and threw a bag together before driving around the edge of the island to Dean's cottage.

When she knocked, he yelled, "Come on in! I figured it was you. The big guy wouldn't have knocked."

He was sitting by the fireplace drinking a beer.

"Are you OK?" he asked.

"Yes, I'm fine," she answered. "How are you? That's the question!"

"I called Gertie down at the general store. She's sorta the nurse around here when all else fails. She's coming to fix my arm until I can get over to the Main tomorrow. I'm drinking as much as I can to get ready," Dean said with a wince.

"The big guy is gone. He took the ferry back," Carolyn responded.

"That big-assed motherfucker!"

"Can I make myself a quick cup of coffee?" she asked. "I have to get away from here tonight. I'm rowing to the Main."

"Ah, not a good idea. Not in the winter," he said. "What in the hell could you have done to rile up that monster? Surely to God, he's not an old boyfriend?"

"No. Hired by the old boyfriend," she answered.

"Well, anyway, it's not a good idea to row over there, not in the winter, and not at night!" Dean scowled.

"I've already been halfway over. If I wait until morning to take the ferry the big guy will be back," Carolyn replied. "My mind is made up."

As she stood up to say goodbye, Dean asked, "Where will you go?"

Carolyn stopped for a moment.

"Somewhere warm. Somewhere far away," she said as her mind wandered. "A place with white sails and soft sand. A safe place."

Her lip quivered and she sniffed as she gave him a quick hug before heading out the door.

Running from Andrew again had brought her here, to this icy island off the coast of Maine. Her frozen fingers rubbed her neck as she remembered the first time he'd hurt her. Returning home hadn't been far enough away from him she'd discovered, after he'd torched her business.

The long winter alone in the isolated cottage had almost allowed her to forget. Almost allowed her to feel safe again.

Almost.

But he'd found her. Or rather sent someone to find her.

Not able to bear thinking of the many betrayals she'd suffered at Andrew's hand, her mind shifted to a happy place. A place where things were easy and bright. She knew she'd be fine. She had money coming from insurance and the sale of her house. She could work again. But right now she needed... She wasn't sure. She hadn't been sure of anything since she'd heard the news of her brother's death.

A scene of white sails and the small picture-postcard ports along the lush Italian coast came to her mind. A snapshot her brother had sent her. A coast far away from trouble. From Andrew.

She'd go to Italy. He'd never find her there. She could start over. There was nothing left for her here.

Yes... Italy...

Cold air burned her lungs as she sighed and looked out over the dark, icy water separating her from the mainland.

CAROL GOODNIGHT

"I need to leave this island now. The hell with the car. The hell with my clothes. My life is worth more than a few thousand dollars."

The smudge-gray sky hung low across the horizon carrying the promise of a new cold front. As she pulled the canoe into the water, a rasping caw echoed across the snow and then on through the silhouette of trees. She listened. Was this the call of the wild? A siren song? An epiphany? Finally? Hard to tell, but she knew what she had to do.

Carolyn Wingate would run again.

Trying to escape the grief after her brother's funeral had only succeeded in one thing; causing more pain. A failed romance, a pathetic love affair, an interlude with a madman? Whatever name you slapped on it, it wouldn't come close to describing her experience.

If she could get away again, perhaps then she could start fresh. The fear and trauma she'd suffered at Andrew's hand would become a painful memory tossed on the smoldering heap with the rest of them. The wealth he'd portrayed had been a sham. He wouldn't try to find her again. Why would he? Now that he'd drained her bank accounts and she was on to him, she was certain he'd move on to the next victim.

Had this been fate? Perhaps things would have been different if she'd kept her gaze right toward the Café Du Monde instead of looking toward Andrew that day. Or maybe if she hadn't been so impressed by his charm. Or if her senses hadn't been so blunted by grief, she might've noticed the darkness about him.

But he was a con. And a good one at that. In time, she would come to realize she'd given herself far too much credit in thinking she could have altered her fate.

Carolyn rowed the canoe to a dark area along the coast, tossed the paddles in the ocean, and stepped out onto the rocky shore. She pulled her identification from her purse, filled it with water, and placed it in the shallows. Waves of emotion washed over her as she picked up a large rock. She mustered strength from beneath her weakness and fear, and bashed the rock against the canoe. She heaved it in the air and brought it down again and again, until her arms trembled. When the front end of the canoe cracked at the joint, she dropped the rock in the surf.

After wrapping her sweater around the seat, she flipped the canoe over and pushed it off shore. She watched it partially submerge as it hung up on the rocks.

"He'll think I'm dead."

A thin smile brightened her face as she realized she'd never felt more alive.

The low beating of a hollow thwup-thwup vibrated against Carolyn's back. The sensation was followed by the sound of a whirring hum and the pulsating rhythm of spinning rotor blades.

The sound intensified as she turned to see the shadow of a helicopter with one faint searchlight rise above the rocky shore. She cocked her head and focused on the black object darting like a giant firefly through the night sky. The machine swooped over the coast and then out to sea. It rose up over the far end of the island near her cottage and then dipped out of sight.

Carolyn reached down and let her fingers linger on the beautiful anklet as she looked up at Witchy Pitchfork in the full moon.

"Open your heart ~ Look within," she whispered before she brushed the hair from her face and started up the cliff.

The End

CAROL GOODNIGHT

A Note from Carol Goodnight

Thank you for reading A Kiss in Darkness. If you enjoyed it, please take a moment to leave a review at your favorite retailer such as Amazon USA. Please check out these other titles by Carol Goodnight.

https://www.amazon.com/Kiss-Darkness-Carolyn-Wingate-Novella-ebook/dp/B06XGPMN9C

BOOK 1 in the Carolyn Wingate Novella Series

A KISS IN DARKNESS

Broken-hearted from her CIA brother's accidental death, Carolyn Wingate, a successful Midwest construction executive, returns from his funeral to find that before his death he'd mailed her a lovely gold-and-diamond chain. Overcome with grief, she runs from everything she's known in a desperate search for solace.

Under the gentle swaying moss in the beguiling city of New Orleans she meets and falls in love with Andrew, a handsome, wealthy blue blood.

But a boat crash in the murky depths of a secluded bayou begins a string of perilous situations where Carolyn finds herself running again.

BOOK 2 in the Carolyn Wingate Novella Series

THE KISS GOODNIGHT

On the run from her crazy ex, Carolyn Wingate finds the gentle waves and sunny shores of the Ligurian Coast of Italy a safe place to begin life again. A new yacht, new friends, and a funny new love almost let her forget the unhinged billionaire that can't seem to let go.

Almost…

https://www.amazon.com/Kiss-Goodnight-Carolyn-Wingate-Novella-ebook/dp/B017XSVUT6

BOOK 3 in the Carolyn Wingate Novella Series

KISS OF THE NAKED LADY

Two sublime seasons have passed and life for Carolyn Wingate couldn't be better. Griff follows her to the vineyard with a marriage proposal and a promise to love and care for her forever.

But the quick report of rifle fire and several bullet wounds set Carolyn on a new path…

A path of revenge.

https://www.amazon.com/Kiss-Naked-Kissed-Night-Novella-ebook/dp/B06XJC32X7

A short story inspired by a character in A KISS IN DARKNESS

LADY CE'CIL

CAROL GOODNIGHT

As Lady Ce'cil strokes the deep scar gashed through her forehead, over her eye, and across her cheek, she slips through time to the stagnate bayous and bald cypress hammocks of South Louisiana. It is in the sweltering summer of 1922 where she achieves fame in the hyperkinetic world of jazz in New Orleans at the sacrifice of love.

https://www.amazon.com/Lady-Cecil-Carol-Goodnight-ebook/dp/B01N4X6W0J

Like my Facebook page ~ Author Carol Goodnight

https://www.facebook.com/Author-Carol-Goodnight-1460852390880142/?hc_ref...

amazon.com/author/carolgoodnight

Made in United States
North Haven, CT
29 May 2024